THE ASSAULT

THE

ASSAULT

REINALDO

ARENAS

Translated by

ANDREW HURLEY

VIKING

VIKING
Published by the Penguin Group
Penguin Books USA Inc., 375 Hudson Street,
New York, New York 10014, U.S.A.
Penguin Books Ltd, 27 Wrights Lane,
London W8 5TZ, England
Penguin Books Australia Ltd, Ringwood,
Victoria, Australia
Penguin Books Canada Ltd, 10 Alcorn Avenue,
Toronto, Ontario, Canada M4V 3B2
Penguin Books (N.Z.) Ltd, 182–190 Wairau Road,
Auckland 10, New Zealand

Penguin Books Ltd, Registered Offices:
Harmondsworth, Middlesex, England

First published in 1994 by Viking Penguin,
a division of Penguin Books USA Inc.

1   3   5   7   9   10   8   6   4   2

Translation copyright © Andrew Hurley and the
Estate of Reinaldo Arenas, 1994. All rights reserved.
Originally published in the Spanish language as *El Asalto* by
Ediciones Universal. © Copyright 1990 by Reinaldo Arenas.
The extract from Aeschylus's *The Libation-Bearers* is from the
translation by E.D.A. Morshead, revised by Moses Hadas
(The George Macy Companies, New York, 1961; Easton Press, 1979).

LIBRARY OF CONGRESS CATALOGING IN PUBLICATION DATA
Arenas, Reinaldo, 1943–1991
[Asalto. English]
The assault / Reinaldo Arenas ; translated by Andrew Hurley.
p.   cm.
ISBN 0–670–84066–1
I. Hurley, Andrew.
PQ7390.A72A813   1994
863—dc20   93–32554

Printed in the United States of America
Set in Adobe Trump Medieval

For Roberto Valero and María Badías,
for having brought back this novel
from the dead . . .

The past is accomplished; but rouse thee to hear
What the future prepareth; awake and appear
Our champion, in wrath and power!

Aeschylus, *The Libation-Bearers*

CONTENTS

1. A View of Mariel   1

2. Of what occurred to Don Quixote with a beautiful huntress   3

3. De Soto's Expedition to Florida   6

4. On the meaning of the colors white and blue   8

5. How a Great Scholar of England Sought to Argue Against Pantagruel and How He Was Overcome by Panurge   11

6. The Metaphors of the *Iliad*   14

7. How the Creator's Wisdom and Providence Shine Greater in Small Things Than in Large Ones   17

8. In which Guzmán de Alfarache tells what befell him once with a beggar that died in Valencia   18

9. Pericles   19

10. The Song of Songs, or the Song of Solomon   21

11. Magellan in India   23

12. The Preeminence of Menelaus   26

13. Transmigration of Souls; Final Beatitude   29

14. The Nestle Tower   31

15. Stone Age remains found in Cuba which are generally classified as Carib Indian in origin but which are not   32

16. How the knights that bore the arms of serpents departed for the kingdom of Gaul and how Fortune cast them down so that by treachery and trickery they were put in great danger of their

lives, being in the power of Arcalus the Enchanter, and also how, freed from that place, they departed in another direction, and how the knights Galaor and Norandel by chance took the same path in search of adventures, and of what befell them 34

17. *A l'ombre des jeunes filles en fleur* 36

18. The Seven Seals of the Song of Alpha and Omega 39

19. Fray Bartolomé de las Casas, His Error 42

20. Victor Hugo's Dream 43

21. On the labor unions of today and Trotsky's errors 44

22. Capital Chapter 46

23. Which recounts the friar's visit to the gardens of the King 50

24. The Vision of Anahuac 61

25. Concerning those things that occurred in Seville up until his embarkation for the Indies 63

26. Letter from José Martí to the Argentine ambassador 66

27. Clocks and Steam Engines 68

28. Prologue and Epilogue 74

29. To the Stars 77

30. Clodio giueth his letter to Auriſtela; the Barbarian Anthony killeth him by miſchance 80

31. Assembly for gathering of withes to be used in tobacco drying, in Pinar del Río 83

32. Fortune Visits Us in Spite of the Rain 84

33. Description of the Temple of the Sun and Its Great Riches 87

34. Hyperion to Belarmino 89

35. Peter Pan Appears 90

36. The Various Kinds of Government and the Ways by Which They Are Established 92

37. A History of the Conspiracies Plotted in Catalonia Against the French Armies ... 93

38. Matanzas' Breadloaf Mountain ... 95

39. Atropos, Clothos, Lachesis, and another Fate (a relatively minor one) not known until today ... 97

40. The Last End ... 101

41. The Four Gods of the Sky According to the Chinese ... 103

42. Thus speak the gods of the Ganges: The great repay no favors of the humble ... 105

43. In which is described the location, size, and shape of the Island ... 107

44. The Part which Divine Providence played in my profession as Author ... 110

45. The terrifying storm that occurred in Guatemala, in which Doña Beatriz de la Cueva lost her life ... 112

46. Jalisco ... 113

47. Of how, because of the great lust which they have, women make love right and left ... 115

48. The Sexual Use of the Anal Orifice ... 118

49. Genetic applications to the yield of various zoogenetic species ... 128

50. On my films ... 131

51. Growing uneasiness. The grandparents and the boat ride at dusk ... 134

52. The Assault ... 135

THE ASSAULT

1

A VIEW OF MARIEL

["*Excursión a Vuelta Abajo*"
Cirilo Villaverde]

The last time I saw my mother, she was out behind the National People's Lumber Cooperative gathering sticks. She was standing with her back to me, bent double, and it looked as though the weight of all those sticks of wood she was carrying was putting a terrible strain on her back. This was my chance; I knew I could not waste a second. I ran straight for her, and I would have killed her, too, but the old bitch must have an eye where her asshole ought to be, because before I could get to her and knock her down and kill her, the old woman whirled around to meet me. She was terrified—oh, but not because of me. She was afraid of the representidial laws and the agents that enforce them, that's what she was afraid of. Because if she had been caught stealing scraps from the National Sawmill, she would have been arrested and tried and sentenced. Which means she would have been killed.

When the old hag turned around, terrified but still as fierce as ever, I saw that dried-out, swollen, diabolic face of hers. I quickly reached down for a stake. I would drive it into her anywhere I could—into her eyes, into her eyes if I could, or if not, into her mouth. And I would push and push, until I saw her teeth come out through the back of her head . . .

She grasped the bundle of sticks in one claw and with the other she started hurling them at me. I picked up a rock that was luckily within reach, and I took careful aim and threw it straight at her chest. She fell backwards onto the ground. I leapt on top of her with the stake, but she kicked me off. I threw myself at her throat, but she opened her mouth, her eyes, and her nose. I looked at her. It had been a long time since I had seen her so close. And then her fangs sank into my neck. I howled. I kicked her in the stomach (or in the knees, I can't be sure) and I broke free. I stumbled off, bleeding and cursing. She picked up the bundle of sticks again and threw the sticks of wood at me one by one, snorting and bellowing. I ran. When I was out of range, I stopped and I turned and started throwing pieces of rusty saw blades at her. *Old bitch, old bitch,* I breathed, but all I could hear was her laughing. What a laugh that woman has. But then the whispering started, and to be on the safe side I left. I did not want to take any chances. *One of these days I'll get you,* I screamed at her with my claws and with my eyes, but without saying a word, listening to the whispering and watching her disappear into the distance, limping a little like she does and laughing or snorting or cursing. The whispering reached its usual pitch, and suddenly the Counter-whispering troops scrambled and the hunt for the whisperer began.

Furious, and still dripping blood from the bite on my neck, I went home. When I got home I looked at myself. The tooth marks were dreadful. But that was not what I was looking at. I was looking at my face. It was the same face, or almost the same, as hers, like a wide flat rock, and in the middle of that expanse of rock, eyes almost bulging out of their sockets. My face was more and more my mother's face. I was coming to look more like her every day, and I still had not killed her. That thought made me even more furious, and frightened as well, so I ran outside again, touching my face with my claws and saying to myself *I'm her, I'm her, and if I don't kill her soon I'll be exactly like her.* I had to find her. So once more I began searching for her, the way I always do, unable to think of anything but finding her and crushing her. But since that day I have not laid eyes on her again. Though I never stop looking.

REINALDO ARENAS

2

OF WHAT OCCURRED TO DON QUIXOTE

WITH A BEAUTIFUL HUNTRESS

[*The Ingenious Gentleman
Don Quixote de la Mancha*
Miguel de Cervantes]

Since I don't live in the Multi-Family, I can get up when I damn well feel like it. Or not go to bed at all. I can do whatever I damn well feel like doing, because I don't live in the Multi-Family. Getting permission not to live in the Multi-Family was not easy. The law states that "All citizens are required to live in the Multi-Family." At first I was taken back to the Multi-Family several times. Like everyone else, I was issued my own place there. Since it was just me and no one else, I was allotted a little over one square yard of floor space, which was the length of my body by the width of my body with my arms at my sides. Other people were assigned more space, because they had a wife or children. At not-night, when the spaces were assigned, there was always someone that tried to take more space than they were issued. If Multi-Family Headquarters found out, the space would be cut down to one-half the original issue, so the person would have to sleep on their side. Of course all you would have to do was inform on someone, even if it was not true, and their space would be cut. One family lost so much space that they all had to sleep stacked on top of an old man, the grandfather, who in turn had to sleep on his side. At the beginning I would inform on people for the fun of it. Then that got boring. So I ran away from the Multi-Family. They hunted me down, and of course they caught me. And they took me back to the Multi. I worked. When they captured me the next time, I had a long list of whisperers. I kept my mouth shut. I added names to the list. The list was something, I'll tell you. I promised to add even more names to it. The only thing I asked, I said, was that I be given permission not to live in the Multi. And they agreed—oh, not at the moment, but later they did. I continued to cooperate. I am now, of course, a member of the Bureau of Counterwhispering, which means that I am a counterwhisperer.

The most unbearable aspect of the Multi-Family was not the floor that you had to sleep on (that in fact you had to live on), it was the other people. You had to sleep with virtually the entire Extended Multi-Family community on top of you. There was always a leg or a navel, a piece of somebody's ugly face or a shock of greasy hair in your face. There were times, looking at the big ear on the gorilla next to me, listening to him breathe, looking at his nose or one of his claws, when I could not take it anymore, it made me vomit. Obviously there is nothing more grotesque than the human body; experience has confirmed that for me. But being required by law to live alongside all those people, being forced to look at their eyes and their tongues and their udders, having to smell their nauseating smells, to step in their disgusting slime, and even having to hear their reckless and absolutely prohibited whispering—I could not bear that. And especially when they would obtain a Breeding Permit and one of them, the female, would start in with that snorting and pawing, that whinnying and drooling, until the other one, the male (who you would think never thought of anything else), would mount her, and then the shaking and wiggling would start, and the wet squishing sounds, and the sickening smells, and then the whinnying and kicking and the spasms and the claws clutching as though one of them were trying to strangle the other one but couldn't quite do it. *That* was the most unbearable aspect of it. I had to escape the Multi-Family or explode—or if I could manage neither of those alternatives, then blow up all the others. That would have been the best thing, but it was much harder. It is always easier to explode, yourself, than to blow everyone else up. It is always a relief to me to see someone explode; it's an even greater relief if I am the one that has brought on the explosion. Someone howls, although howling is strictly prohibited. That is another reason I became a counterwhisperer—now I can have many more people blown up than I could before.

Sometimes when someone passes too close to me, it makes me boil inside, and I can feel myself about to turn, leap, tear their throat out—those legs, that snout, those hairs in their nose enrage me—but I control myself. My tongue quivers, I feel hot slaver dripping from my fangs, but I control myself. I am waiting for my mother.

3

DE SOTO'S EXPEDITION TO FLORIDA

[*Historia general de las Indias*
Francisco López de Gómara]

So I return home, or rather return to the place I live. I live in a glass house, but it is actually just *called* a glass house. It is called that because it can be destroyed whenever the Office of the Represident so orders, but in fact it is made out of old cans and pieces of cardboard and sticks of wood and grappling irons and hooks and rocks and pieces of glass and barbed wire from the last big war. The entire surface of my glass house is covered with sharp edges and pointed spikes and twisted strands of wire. Mold and mildew and time have turned everything slightly green.

When it gets dark, I take up my post. Soon some airborne animal (one of the few that have survived) flies into the hooks and grappling irons and gets caught. I can hear its fluttering and flapping about even from inside my house, and the more it flaps and struggles the more hooks it is impaled on. Blood drips in through the chinks. The animal shrieks. I go outside. This time it's a snowy egret, or maybe it's a sea gull. Yes, I think it's a sea gull. *Sea gull, sea gull,* I say, as I climb up the wall of my glass house to retrieve it. The bird beats its wings and looks at me hopefully. In its eyes I can see myself, or at least I can see a piece of my face, which means I see my mother's face. I hold the bird down with my claw and I scrape it back and forth across the shards and slivers of glass. Even after it is gutted it still kicks once or twice. I eat. It is food for a king. That scum that lives in the Multi-Family will never taste such a deli-

REINALDO ARENAS

cacy. The part of the bird I most enjoy crushing with my teeth is its head, and the part of the head I like best is its eyes. That was where I saw her, just a moment ago. My mother's face—my face. And I still have not managed to kill her. I go outside again. It's a starry night, as they used to say, way back in the past. What that phrase means is that the sky is full of all sorts of rubbish, or trash, or junk —furies that go flashing by shooting sparks and sputters. Some of them are larger, others smaller—how the hell should I know what they're all called.

And what do I *care* what's going on up there. If I go outside it certainly is not to look at all that hubbub and confusion up there, it's only because I cannot bear to be inside anymore, when I know that my mother is out there somewhere, laughing at me, while I am coming to look more and more like her every day. Now I am out in the middle of this huge open clearing, under that sputtering, sparkling sky. *If I could only find her tonight,* I say, and my fingers are now becoming long, menacing, knotty, as they transform into claws. *If only I could get my claws in her throat tonight.* And now my claws cannot bear it any longer, and they reach out and make savage arabesques in the air. *If only I could strangle her tonight, this very night,* I say, and I start walking. *It's all right, it's him, it's the ruthless one,* one Counterwhispering agent says to another who is about to stop me and ask for identification. They snap to attention and salute me. And I continue my search.

4

ON THE MEANING OF THE COLORS

WHITE AND BLUE

[Gargantua and Pantagruel
François Rabelais]

I've always hated my mother, of course. As long as I've
known her, that is. At first my hatred for the cow came in
fits and starts. Then it was always there. One day I saw
myself in a mirror and I noticed that there was something
about me that reminded me of her. I looked at myself a
while later and it seemed to me I was starting to resemble
her. I looked at myself again, and I had the same sensation,
and then not long after that, when I examined myself a
fourth time, I could clearly see that I was coming to look
more and more like the damned woman. And after that, my
hatred was no longer just *there* anymore—it began to grow.
It was then that I began looking at myself all the time, and
at last I could see, more clearly every day, that everything
about me was beginning to look just like her—my eyes, my
ears, my paws, and my snout were becoming virtually *hers*.
I was slowly but surely changing away from myself and
changing into her. So of course I realized (and now the fact
is more obvious to me every day) that if I didn't kill her
soon, I would *be* her, I would actually turn into her, and
then, being her, how would I ever be able to kill her? So I
made my decision—I grabbed the Multi-Family knife (because at the time, we were living in the Multi) and ran over
to where the filthy whore was washing the communal overalls (because once a week, one member of the Extended

Multi-Family has to wash all the overalls), and I was about to stab her in the back, no matter what might happen to me as a result—anything was better than letting her go on living, which meant letting her swallow me whole, kill me, even say that I was a whisperer, which of course would be all it would take to do away with me forever—but the god-damned she-mule turned around, brayed like a donkey over the communal laundry vat, and, denting every drum and can in her way, fled madly out into the not-park. *Murderer,* she screamed as she wildly ran through the not-park, *murrr-der-er! He's trying to kill his own mother! Get him, get him! He's trying to ki-i-i-ll me!* I was seized and tied up to the big stake in the center of the not-park. But I knew how to defend myself. I said she had kicked a dent in the People's Communal Washtub that belonged to all of us in the Extended Multi-Family. *She dented it on purpose,* I added, *screaming insults against the Represident.* She denied it, of course, but it was true that as she was trying to get away she had put a nick in the enamel of the People's Vat. Since the Represident himself had invented this method of laundry, her crime was Destruction of Communal Property in the First Degree, and punishable by death. She was seized and about to be carried off to be tortured—although the members of the Multi-Family wanted to exterminate her on the spot—but agents from Higher Authority, without a word of explanation, took charge of her.

I later heard that she had not confessed (though I find this inexplicable) and that nothing had happened to her (which if true is even more difficult to understand). According to my sources, the reason for this is that she herself is a member of Counterwhispering. When I was told *that,* I realized (as who would not?) that if one wants to survive, the best thing one can do is become an agent for the Bureau of Counterwhispering, and so within a week I had informed on and captured more than a hundred whisperers. I personally caught them and put the ring around their neck and dragged them off to the Cells on Wheels and saw that they were brought before the People's Court of Justice and Execution. I even offered to perform the executions myself.

So I am a counterwhisperer. I can walk around, and I can leave the Represidential Capital any time I please (with proper authorization). I can talk, I can whisper and say it was the idiot next to me that did it and screw him, which is most enjoyable. And of course I get two ladles-ful from the Communal Cauldron. But my mother is still alive, and I am still coming more and more to look like her. I became a counterwhisperer so that I could hunt her down and liquidate her wherever I found her. What comes after that, I will have to wait and see. But until the moment comes when I have completed my task, I am on constant prowl. I shall not rest. *It's him, it's the mad counterwhisperer*, one agent says to another as I pass by. And I know that their eyes continue to follow me, even after I have passed the checkpoint; somewhat baffled, they are still watching me. In order to show the agents some justification for my rage, I promise myself that today the cells of every Communal Prison will be packed full of whisperers.

5

HOW A GREAT SCHOLAR OF ENGLAND

SOUGHT TO ARGUE AGAINST PANTAGRUEL

AND HOW HE WAS OVERCOME BY PANURGE

[Gargantua and Pantagruel
François Rabelais]

The sun has begun to crackle on the sharp metal barbs of the not-benches in the not-park. Throughout every corner of the Represidential Capital resounds the morning represidential anthem, which is played, of course, in honor of our great Represident. This morning, like every other, the anthem trumpets everyone out of bed and off to the factories and the fields. The day's light shines brighter and brighter. I pee and I vomit a little behind a not-bench, next to some of the vermin that have been snared on the hooks during the not-night. Then I immediately get into line to make a bus; I hook my elbows into the next person's, and the next person hooks his into the next person's, and so on, and when there are seventy-five of us, the man in charge of transport yells *Full up!* cracks his whip once, and the bus, which is all of us hooked into an Indian file by our elbows, takes off. We march. My closest bus-segment is an old man who looks down at the ground and then looks up at me. *What's your problem, you old asshole, you old monkey, you old faggot?* I scream at him with my eyes. The old man appears not to understand me, or perhaps appears to understand me perfectly, because he stops looking at me. He gets off in the first uncoupling. I also get off. The morning represidential anthem ends, and a wave of pre-applause welcomes the *Good morning, my sons and daughters* that emerges from all the loudspeakers, the voice of our great Represident. Then there is the morning represidential address. Then comes the usual wave of post-applause. But suddenly, in the midst of the applause, there is a whisper, a genuine whisper. I run—I must not let him get away. Behind me, others are running too, people trying to earn merit points. I won't allow that, I won't allow them to better me. I whisper myself, and then I sink my claws into the little boy that's running along behind me—*Oh, so it's you, you little bastard!* The little boy protests. I squeeze his throat as fast as I can and his protest turns into a whisper. *Oh, so you're still . . .* Beating and kicking him, I lead him (he already has the iron collar around his neck) to the first Cell on Wheels, lock him up, and outside on the blackboard I write my counterwhisperer number. I want everyone to know that I was the morning's hero. Our great Represident's glorious greeting is repeated again by the loudspeakers, meaning that we should all be on our marks, or at our lines, or in our centers or circles or production shifts— *Good morning, my sons and daughters.*

The words, I don't know why, remind me that I still have not come across my mother. My rage mounts. Muttering, I stalk down the absolutely deserted street. My spirits are soothed for a few moments as I watch officers from the Post-Mortuary Prison carry away the bodies of people snagged during the not-night on the hooks on the not-benches in the not-park. The idea of the not-park with its not-benches covered with barbs came, of course, from our great Represident. The malcontents and disaffected sectors of society tend to indulge in idleness, and they unconsciously indict themselves when they sit on a not-bench (the only public seating there is), because they're hooked on the barbs and capture-killed at the same time. A noble and heroic task indeed is performed by this grand represidential invention. I go over to one of the not-benches, and

I start unhooking the hooks from some people that were caught-killed like a swarm of flies by flypaper. I drag them off to the post-mortuary cells. I lock them up, and I scrawl my number on the blackboard. Workwise, it has not been a bad morning.

6

THE METAPHORS OF THE *ILIAD*

[*La civilización griega*
(Author forgotten)]

It is now noon, and the efforts of the Nation's loyal beasts are redoubled. The sun sears the backs of the swinish herd that begins its counter-siesta by picking up litter—rocks, pieces of cardboard from placards and signs, cans from who knows how long ago—and carrying it all to the not-park. Then, when they have carried all the trash there, they scatter it again. And even more euphorically they launch themselves once more into the trash collection. And when the counter-siesta is over and it's time to go back to work, one by one they hook elbows and make the bus that carries them back to their production line, circle, factory, or branch. I examine them closely, one by one, although by now I know practically every one of them—gaunt, weary-looking mules, bony geldings, pigs with tousled, matted hair, or none at all. The whelps are the most horrible: in their heavy, ill-fitting multi-overalls, they look like nothing so much as clumsy turtles crawling aimlessly around in shells too big for them. One of these supposed children trips when another kid that's trying to get ahead of him steps on his multi-overall. Hundreds of naked feet walk across him. Finally he stands up and makes the first segment of the next bus.

I take the last bus, after I have made sure to observe them all. My mother was not among them. The sun is now baking the beasts, and from their skin comes that nauseating stench that they, of course, cannot smell. I can smell it because I am not always with them. The bus is now going through a muddy stretch of road. Their feet paddle harder, their elbows squeeze tighter, their knees sink in, and they strain not to bog down. The last segment pushes the one in front of it, the one in front pushes the one in front of *it*, and so on down the line, and at last the bus manages to emerge from the swamp. At exactly the stroke of the hour, the workers reach their production lines. Now they all get off. (Now they all pretend they get off.) There is not a sound, and their muzzles are all caked with mud. Some of them, the youngest ones, those that have never taken a real bus, really get off, they actually get off the bus. The others, the few who know what a real bus was, prefer not to remember; they know what remembering will cost them, and so all they remember is our great Represident's words: *Memory is diversionist, and must be dealt with harshly. Maximum punishment.* Now I am one of them, I take a position behind that old cow with huge vacant eyes. Does this old cow remember buses? I wonder. Is she my mother? I wonder. I look at her closely and I touch my face. No, that is not my face yet. The line moves along quickly. It's nutrifamily time. No one ever fails to make this line. If my mother is anywhere in the Represidential Capital, she has to come here. The woman with the cow's eyes seems to tremble with emotion and excitement as she moves slowly closer to the bucket where the nutrifamily water is boiling. I am constantly watching the faces. Some people are already eating—without speaking, as regulations require. Most of them, like the old cow, their lips quivering, are emotional; they are moved and grateful. I look down the waiting, eager line. I wish I could go down this line, one by one, slitting their throats. The last one, the one in front of him, the one whose body strains forward there, all of them, all of them. Might not my mother be here, in disguise? This sickening old man here, might he not be my mother? No, disguises are not allowed. I must control myself. I must pull myself together. I must not abuse my freedom. I must try to marshal all my strength, for if I am to destroy her, her above all, my mother—whom I resemble more every day—I will need all my strength. *What do the rest of these animals mean to you? Enjoy yourself at their expense if you want to,* I tell myself, *but don't put yourself at risk by overzealousness. . . .* So I stand quietly in the long line. But when the big trembling cow stands before the bucket at last, when she takes out her counter-siesta member's card, with her hours worked on it, with her unfailing attendance at the Represidential Square, at the Grand National Patriotic Plaza, I start whispering, softly, *like this,* almost imperceptibly, with my lips squeezed tight together, the way I have done so many times before. And as I do, the man wielding the ladle lets out a curse. *Long live our glorious Represident!* he shouts, and he turns over the bucket. The moaning cow, who was already stretching out her bowl toward the ladler and preparing her grimace of thanks, howls in horror.

Whore, criminal, I yell at her, grabbing her by the throat. And amidst the euphoria of all those beasts from whom the whispering has snatched away their nutribroth, I administer summary justice to her with my special-issue Claw of Power. The cries and insults against the criminal are deafening.

At last, to restore order, I climb on top of the cadaver (on which I have carved my number—another merit point for me) and cry *Long live our glorious Represident!*

To production! I cry. And to thundering huzzahs and hurrahs, the beasts march off to their production lines. *Hurrah!* I shout again, laughing and thinking *At least none of those beasts marching back to work shrieking* (among them, me) *will eat today.*

7

HOW THE CREATOR'S WISDOM
AND PROVIDENCE SHINE GREATER IN
SMALL THINGS THAN IN LARGE ONES

[Introducción al símbolo de la fe
Fray Luis de Granada]

Still hungry, the beasts have made up the bus to return to the Multi-Family. I almost enjoy looking at them now. Listening to the rumbling of their gut. And hearing the cheers that issue from their lips. I like to see those dry faces watching each other, noting for possible future use the number of bravos every other face yells. I look at the herd of sheep, and as they know they are being watched, they bleat all the louder. And I can't stop laughing. I almost laugh out loud. And the bravos grow louder and louder.

All afternoon, the cows and the castrated hogs have worked feverishly. There is tremendous tension in the air; they all know that because of the whispering in the Multi-Family line, any negligence will be severely dealt with. Although the truth is that most of them work not because they fear reprisal but simply because they are degenerate beasts.

8

IN WHICH GUZMÁN DE ALFARACHE

TELLS WHAT BEFELL HIM ONCE WITH A

BEGGAR THAT DIED IN VALENCIA

[*Guzmán de Alfarache*
Mateo Alemán]

"Degenerate beasts" is right. A natural beast would never work so long, so hard, and so unresistingly.

9

PERICLES

[*Parallel Lives*
Plutarch]

What I find most repulsive about them is that rank smell
of old urine, of stagnant shit that they give off. Their bodies
have an odor of carrion about them, of something dead—
though not completely dead, more like meat suffering an
ongoing, eternal suppuration. I have noticed that they have
different stenches—when you are a few feet away they have
one smell, and from farther away another, and when you
are standing directly beside them they smell another way
entirely—worse, of course. On second thought, though,
what I probably detest most about them is not their stench
at all, but the fact that their heads are generally shaved,
their necks are broad and bluish-colored where the sweat
collects, and their eyes never fill their sockets. Plus their
eyelids are always half closed, because they know that if
they open their eyes completely they could offend some
agent. Those eyes that are always staring at the tip of the
hoof they walk on, or at nothing at all. But no, that is not
it either—what I detest most about them is their bones, the
bones of an old monkey covered with long ropelike veins
that always look as though they are about to pop. When
they walk, when they clatter and jerk along, when they use
their front claws to pick up something, something they are
required to transport—how furious it makes me to hear
that creaking, how hard it is to control myself, how hard
not to crush them. Now, to the sound of the anthem announcing that the bright-and-glorious-day has ended and

the not-night has begun, I watch them digging a hole, bending over, scratching and scrabbling to obey the law of not-
rest, and all one can hear is the *scrape-scrape-scrape* of the
bones they drag along. So hateful, so abominable. *Scrape-
scrape-scrape.*

10

But no, that's not it either. Even more abominable, even more disgusting, is seeing how sometimes, when they are back in the Multi-Family, and they have scratched their signatures on the request and received their Breeding Permit, they twine themselves around each other in the act of patriotic procreation. The coupling begins with whimpers and moans and kicks, and sometimes traded blows with clenched claws, and posturing on all fours. Finally they mount each other. The female, who pretends that she is a dog, rubs against the hog. The male, who for a moment looks as though he is about to wring the female's neck, at last massages her breastbone and tosses her about, making a terrible racket and stirring up the other cockroaches (who look on, sweaty and shiny, though since they have not received their own Breeding Permits they may not themselves poke at or hook onto each other). Finally the male, who is acting the part of the scorpion, plunges his barbed sting into the spider, and the spider screams. And with that, the male kicks at the female all the harder. Their bones clatter, and from both of them there issue a rank, hot smell and an oozing slime. Then they lie still for a while, stupefied and making low grumbling sounds, until the period authorized by the Breeding Permit ends (generally half an hour) and the supervising agents pull them apart. What is almost incredible is that when the two beasts begin oozing slime and intertwining with each other, they will not separate or stop making that typical muted grumbling sound they make, even if someone throws acid on them or tries to set them afire with gasoline. That is the truth, as incredible as it may seem. I have tried it, and I know.

11

MAGELLAN IN INDIA

[*Magellan*
Stefan Zweig]

During the not-night shift I only kick a few beasts and then I leave. When I get home to my glass house I stop to think, and I realize that among that entire army of vermin that I have been observing day after day, not one of them is my mother. That means I have to leave the Represidential Capital and look elsewhere. I go to Counterwhispering Headquarters. I identify myself and I am allowed to enter. *I want to leave, I want to travel,* I say, and because I sense that the Counterwhispering Officer at the front desk still has some misgivings, I explain exactly what it is I want: *I want to kill my mother,* I tell him, *but I haven't been able to find her.* The Counterwhispering Officer looks at me impassively and hands me a form to fill out. At the end of it, in the space for General Observations, I write: *I suspect that my mother is the leader of the Whispering Conspiracy.*

I am shown into another waiting room. There I am greeted by the second-in-command of the Counterwhispering Corps. He orders me to take a seat. He's an old man, more than eighty years old. A great fighter in the struggle.

"Long live our glorious Represident!" he cries out to me in greeting, when I sit down. "Speak," he then says to me.

Going straight to the point, I explain to him that I want to eliminate my mother. "If I don't get rid of her soon," I add, "I'll eliminate myself, and you and your corps will be the loser if that happens."

The old man looks at me.

"Long live our glorious Represident!" he cries again. I know that these exclamations are not directed at me, they're for the benefit of the bugs that the place is crawling with. "Who knows," he says then, and it strikes me that he has made a halfhearted attempt at a sigh but then thought better of it. "Yours is a personal, not a family matter. What does the Multi-Family care whether you kill your mother or not."

I explain once again that I suspect her of being the leader of the Whispering Conspiracy.

"Long live our glorious Represident! Prove to me that she is even a member of the Whispering Conspiracy, not to mention the leader, and I promise you that I will find her for you personally," he says, and stretching his thick lips into a kind of a smile, he adds, "Prove it to me."

"But what does Headquarters care whether I kill her or not, after all? I'm one of your best agents. And I'm getting better every day. The problem is that until I eliminate her, I can't really keep my mind on my work. I know that she's following me, I know it. . . . All I ask is that you search the lists of all the Multi-Families and the directories of the Re-presidential Capital, the Servo-Perimeters, and the Satellite Cities. It wouldn't take long."

"Your mission would have some merit if it served some Multi-Family purpose . . ."

"But my mother . . ."

"Long live our glorious Represident! Your mother is not an agent in the Whispering Conspiracy," he says to me now, angrily, and then he calms down again. "Before granting you this audience I spoke with the High Secretary. Here is your checkpoint pass. It is good for six months. But you are to go on a patriotic mission, not a personal one. We want this whispering eliminated. We want applause when it's ordered and shouting when it's ordered. Not one whisper more, not one, and not a word that has not been approved by Pre-Planning. You must obey these instructions, which have been sent down directly from the Office of the

Supreme Represident through the High Secretary. You may go now.

"Oh, and about your mother—she is of no interest to us. We are simply interested in using your hate, properly channeled, for the purposes of the Nation. On the other hand," he now says paternally to me, "kill her if you want. The High Secretary has not prohibited that."

"Long live the Supreme Represident!" I reply, and I head for the bunker at the checkpoint.

12

THE PREEMINENCE OF MENELAUS

[The *Iliad*
Homer]

I come to the first checkpoint. Immediately, the guards turn their guns on me. Without speaking, as the rules prescribe, I take out my papers, the authorizations scribbled out by the Supreme Represident's personal High Secretary. Now the guards at the checkpoint frisk me and search the blue overalls I have worn for this occasion—the same blue overalls the rest of the people that live here wear. One soldier, who seems to be the leader of the guard, clumsily flourishes a clipboard. Then I am subjected to the interrogation, which goes something like this: The soldier interrogating me slowly reads a list of questions. He notes down my answer with an "X" in the blank provided. Then there are various howls and barks, some goose-stepping and clicking of heel talons, the mandated shouting of "Long live our glorious Represident," and finally I am allowed to pass through the checkpoint.

Now I am on the other side of the barrier, outside the Represidential Capital, i.e., in the first Servo-Perimeter. It is the hour for the not-rest period. The nutrifamily period is over and all personnel, following the instructions contained in the manual of the Represidential Code, are talking out loud. Therefore everyone is screaming. I notice (because the truth is, it has been months since the last time I came through the gate into one of these Perimeters) that in the Servo-Perimeter, unlike the Represidential Center (by which I mean, of course, the Represidential Capital), people

REINALDO ARENAS

constantly wave their paws about, and everyone seems stupider, the beasts and vermin all flapping about in their standard-issue blue overalls, and with their heads shaved. They all wiggle their ass more—when they walk, of course, but when they are just standing still, as well. At this very minute, for example, I've got my eye on that group over there; of course it *is* the hour authorized for shrieking, but be that as it may, there is much more ass-shaking, noise, and general racket, and the overall level of obstreperousness is higher than in the Represential Capital. There, things are slower, and grayer too; here, everything is red-colored, and faster-moving. Backside-wiggling seems to be performed with a certain high-spiritedness, even with a degree of authenticity. I look at that couple over there, I move a bit closer (shaking my ass the way they do, the way everyone does), and I observe them. Sometimes, like them, I walk on all fours, or I stand, the way they do, on the tips of my claws. And I continue to wiggle my backside as I observe the natives of this Perimeter.

Look—that mare over there shrieking at the top of her lungs might be my mother. Still wiggling my rear end, I circle around until I'm face-to-face with her snout. The disgusting she-mule, standing there beside another verminous insect, has the unheard-of gall to smile at me. The disgust and revulsion I feel is so overwhelming that I cannot even examine her. I go to the far side of the authorized zone and vomit. *But what if that animal were my mother!* I ask myself. So I go back into that wriggling, writhing mass; skipping on all fours, I caper over to the same couple.

"Heow, heow," I say.

And the vermin-cunt looks at me again. I look straight at her this time, straight into her face, knowing that there is no risk in this, since there is nothing left inside me to vomit up. This time she not only smiles, but still swaying her backside she takes one of my claws and urges me to shake myself as well. I wriggle so that I can observe her, so that I can touch her. I touch her horrible white smooth face.

My skin crawls as I feel her skin. Then she smiles again. I glare at her in fury. She keeps smiling. If one feature of her face, if a single feature reminded me of my mother, I would strangle her this very instant, but she is tall and thin, and she has eyelashes, and her mouth, incredibly, contains all her teeth. The teeth, moreover, gleam. . . . All I would have to do, if this one resembled my mother in the least, is whisper softly, and then take her neck, and squeeze . . . I put my hands around her neck, which does not in the least resemble my mother's. She smiles. Maybe she thinks I am going to caress her. My claws begin to squeeze. I see her large eyes open wide, gazing on me in ecstasy. And at that instant there is an enormous *Clang!* announcing that the backside-moving hour is over and that the period for mechanized labor, the *Ga-ga-boom* period, has begun. Everyone stops swaying, and all the animals pick up their equipment, gear, and tools for work. Everyone stands rigidly at attention. And then, elbows all linked, they depart for the work area assigned to them for this particular not-night. The she-animal touched my claw for one instant, and then she turned and looked at me again, and I even think she made some sort of sign to me as she was forming up the bus. The filthy whore.

13

TRANSMIGRATION OF SOULS;

FINAL BEATITUDE

[*The Divine Comedy*
Dante Alighieri]

The work of this entire Servo-Perimeter, as for many of the rest of them, consists of picking up all the outdated placards, posters, signs, flags, and so on, and chewing them up into a sort of paste or viscous mass, mixing that paste with other ingredients (excrement, blood), and then turning it into placards, posters, signs, flags, and so on. The work, hard enough in and of itself, is much more difficult these days because the Grand Anniversary is at hand. The Grand Anniversary of our glorious Represident, called the Represiversary for short, is one of a number of glorious communal commemorations of the rise of the Supreme Represident, and naturally every energy is dedicated to the manufacture of the millions of commemorative articles (flags, pins, posters, and so on) that will be employed to honor it.

Everyone works passionately. Every ten hours a halt is called so that an anthem in honor of the Supreme Represident can be intoned. I make my way through the crowds of people, looking at every face, observing, examining, scrutinizing. Now they are bending over and picking up, now chewing, now spitting into the huge sack. The process is perfectly choreographed: while they are not chewing, which is to say while they are bending over, the immense crowd of beasts cries *Long live our glorious Supreme Represident!*

and then at once they begin chewing their pasty cuds. Silence (for now they are chewing and spitting into the huge sack). Then, as with one voice, deafening cheers are shouted out once more, as the beasts then bend over and pick up the litter. I look at them one by one—as they bend over, as they chew, as they turn their heads and spit, as they bend over again, and as, bent double, they once more shout their hurrahs. No, none of them is my mother. The damned woman is not here either.

14

THE NESTLE TOWER

[*Gaspard de la nuit*
Aloysius Bertrand]

An accident. Kicking and jostling. One man has tripped on another man's multi-overalls and fallen. All the rest walk on inexorably, with their huge sacks over their shoulders, murmuring the Represidential Hurrah, picking up litter and chewing on it, and trampling the beast that now lies dying under their feet. The next rank, and the rank following that, and all the ranks farther back, go on walking over him, digging the talons of their back claws into him, picking up litter, chewing, and spitting into the huge sack slung over their backs. Nothing remains of the miserable wretch.

15

STONE AGE REMAINS FOUND IN CUBA

WHICH ARE GENERALLY CLASSIFIED

AS CARIB INDIAN IN ORIGIN

BUT WHICH ARE NOT

[*"Las cuatro culturas indias de Cuba"*
Fernando Ortiz]

What if that number that fell and was crushed to a bloody pulp and then compacted—what if that number was my mother? If it was, I will now be doomed to spend the rest of my life in the pursuit of something that does not exist but that, since I cannot be sure whether it exists or not, will be constantly gnawing at me, destroying me—because the important thing is not that my mother be dead but that I *know* she is dead, and that it was I myself that killed her. Because only the fact that I myself have destroyed her will allow me to savor the full certainty that she is, in fact, destroyed. She knows that I am hunting her, and so she knows that only if she pretends to be dead will I ever stop. That, in fact, is an excellent strategy for anyone that feels persecuted or hunted—pretend to be wiped out, annihilated, liquidated, so that the other person, if he is the usual idiot (and ninety-nine percent of hunters *are* the usual idiots), will stop the search, and then the hunted person can jump out behind the hunter's back and *Zap!*—the hunted kills the hunter, and can return to his life. But I know that she is almost certainly still alive, and so I never stop moving my eyes, swiveling my head about on my neck, looking

REINALDO ARENAS

for her. I cannot allow her to remain alive while I am. I cannot allow *her* to annihilate *me*. Before all else, I cannot accept the idea that she has been eliminated. And especially, or before all else, or first of all, or more than anything, or whatever the hell it is one says in these situations, I also cannot accept that it may be someone else that destroys her, and not I, or accept that she may have destroyed herself. That would be the worst thing that could happen to me. Because if that were to happen, how could I prove to myself that she is dead, that she no longer exists, that she is gone, how could I make her not live, not exist in my imagination and in my fear? Therefore it has to be *me* that finds her and crushes her, that finds her and kills her. Otherwise—whether she is crushed or not, killed or not, dead or not, so long as I am unaware of her destruction— it will be *she* who finally destroys *me*. And I, horror of horrors, will then become her.

16

HOW THE KNIGHTS THAT BORE THE ARMS OF SERPENTS DEPARTED FOR THE KINGDOM OF GAUL AND HOW FORTUNE CAST THEM DOWN SO THAT BY TREACHERY AND TRICKERY THEY WERE PUT IN GREAT DANGER OF THEIR LIVES, BEING IN THE POWER OF ARCALUS THE ENCHANTER, AND ALSO HOW, FREED FROM THAT PLACE, THEY DEPARTED IN ANOTHER DIRECTION, AND HOW THE KNIGHTS GALAOR AND NORANDEL BY CHANCE TOOK THE SAME PATH IN SEARCH OF ADVENTURES, AND OF WHAT BEFELL THEM

[*Amadis of Gaul*
(Anonymous)]

Therefore, the first thing I must do is avoid the possibility that someone besides me gets to my mother before I do and annihilates her. For if I let that happen, there will be no escape for me. Therefore, what I must first do is look for her where she runs the greatest risk of being destroyed, in the Concentrated Rehabilitation Camps, in the National

REINALDO ARENAS

Communal Prisons, or in the Theater of Retractations. Quickly, before they liquidate her—liquidate her myself. Because if she is anywhere else, sooner or later I will be able to find her, but if she is in one of those places, I will never be able to find her once she is dealt with. Idiot, get going.

17

A L'OMBRE DES JEUNES FILLES EN FLEUR

[Marcel Proust]

I must await the coming of not-night in order to request permission to enter the National Communal Prison. Before not-nightfall it is impossible, because every official in the Servo-Perimeter is occupied full-time with the counting, checking, rechecking, re-counting, and counter-checking of the residents. The count is performed here, as it is in other Servo-Perimeters and Satellite Cities, as well as in the Re-presidential Capital itself, in the following way: The insect (that is, the cow or the castrated hog), with its number on its back, must file, in numerical order, past the account-ants. It is all quite fast. The accountant looks at the hog's back and scribbles in his notebook. If a beast should be absent, the next piece of vermin must present the absent beast's identification card and individual multi-overall, which it turns in to one of the accountant's assistants; in the notebook, the reason for the absence is noted. The only possible reason: *Treason.* Because in this society, as the Su-preme Represent has repeatedly stated, getting sick is treason—one of the worst sorts of treason, in fact, and so whenever I find some sick number I quote our glorious Re-president's speech about that crime verbatim as I throw the sick animal into the Cell on Wheels. I am absolutely con-vinced that becoming sick is a terrible act of treason. Can a sick number work for the common good? And is Not Working for the Common Good not one of the worst crimes that one of our brothers or sisters can commit? But then how are we to distinguish the truly sick number from the

REINALDO ARENAS

number that is merely malingering, merely pretending to be sick? Yet how can we not consider even the genuinely sick number a traitor, since it has allowed itself to be undermined by illness even as it lives in the purest and healthiest society that has ever existed or ever will exist? And worse, the sick number's treason—is it not a treason that creeps through the Nation, infecting others . . . ?

And so I stop beside one of the great metal cages and I observe the count as I used to do every day in the Represidential Capital. But none of these numbers passing by is my mother. I take out the little sliver of mirror that I am still allowed to have, thanks to my position as counterwhisperer, and I look at myself again. And I look at the cows passing by, but no, none of them is my mother. Then I walk over toward the main offices of the National Communal Prison.

It is a very dark not-night. Unlike the not-night in the Represidential Capital, where there are always some spotlights on in the not-park, here all the lights are used to light the checkpoints. The idea of the not-night (like all authentically brilliant ideas) was the Supreme Represident's. I can recall the speech introducing the concept as though it were yesterday: *How,* the Represident scolded, *can one imagine night existing in our society? No—we cannot accept that. We therefore abolish night.* And on that day he created the not-night, all during which, and even more so during the glorious day, we are exhorted to keep up our work and maintain our optimism. *We abolish from the language, from our memory, and from the world . . . all those decadent and anti-vital concepts that we have inherited from the reactionary past. We shall optimize the language as we have optimized life itself.* Thus he created the not-night. . . .

I am so wrapped up in my dramatic re-creation of that speech that I bump into the side of a Cell on Wheels and almost crack my skull. The blow to my head is hard, but naturally those famous words of the Supreme Represident immediately come to my mind: *What blow can make a dent in our iron optimism!* Those words raise me to my feet again. Once more standing, I realize that a sort of moan is coming from inside. There is a prisoner in there. I peer through the bars, and I see it. It is a boy. I stagger back in disgust and revulsion. The boy moans. Incredibly, his head is not shaved; in fact, he has a great deal of hair. I do not have to ask what his crime is. It is obvious. When I put my claw in to hit him across the eyes, my skin touches his hair and my skin crawls. The sensation is so nauseating that I step back. What is truly incredible about this is that the Management of this Servo-Perimeter would allow a person to let his hair grow so long. There is no denying that a Servo-Perimeter, no matter how well managed it may be, is not the Represidential Capital, where there is the constant presence of the Supreme Represident to keep everything under control. In these outlying regions, among the Servo-Perimeters and Satellite Cities, my mother might be able to survive. These are the places where I must search for her.

18

THE SEVEN SEALS

OF THE SONG OF ALPHA AND OMEGA

[*Thus Spake Zarathustra*
Friedrich Nietzsche]

My mother's ears are large, rough-skinned, and stick out
from the side of her head as far as a giant bat's, or a rat's,
or a dog's, or an elephant's, or any other fucking animal's
you can think of, and they are always pricked up. Her eyes
are round, revolving bug-eyes, like a rat's or a frog's, or
whatever the fuck other kind of disgusting, nervous,
twitching little animal you can think of. Her nose is like
the beak of some furious bird; her snout, or trunk, is very,
very long, but round at the same time. It reminds you of a
dog's or a boa constrictor's, or—but let someone else try
to describe the fucking thing, it makes me sick to think
about it. Her neck is short, and it swivels like the neck
of an owl or a squashed egret or the devil only knows
what other kind of strange beast. And her body (which
every time I come across her seems to have become even
more inflated and shapeless, wrapped as it is in its un-
varying blue monkey-suit of a multi-overall) is massive,
powerful, barrel-chested, potbellied, bulging, vast, noxious-
smelling, hairy in some parts, sickly white and bald in
others, and totally shameless. Her walk is like a fucking
pole's would be, if a pole could walk—a furious, angry
thing strutting about stiffly, and giving the impression
that for all she cares the world can fuck itself. It is the
walk of a person with hives who is about to go off the

deep end and explode, but who never quite does explode. The last time I saw her it seemed to me that when she moved there was a sort of *pff, pff* sound she made. Maybe she was whispering, the miserable bitch. And I didn't manage to strangle her. What I do not understand is how she can maintain that size of hers, that body like a two-ton mare, that weight, when—by official decree—anyone that exceeds the strict weight limit (which is basically skin and bones) is sent off to be rigorously interrogated and, should theft from the communal stores be involved, is almost always executed. Sometimes, of course, the swelling of the body indicates that the person is actually ill, and therefore a double traitor, "because the person both stops producing *and* infects the rest . . ." It is very strange, my mother's case. Or might it be that she was wearing another rag of an overall on top of the rag of the official multi-overall? . . . I look at myself. I touch myself. I touch my trunk (or snout), I touch my long, broad ears, I run my hands over my belly and squeeze it a little, here there is hair, there there is none. My garment is the regulation multi-overall. I am her, I am almost exactly *her*. I run terrified through the Counterwhispering troops that are shooting their guns up into the not-night, in honor of the Supreme Represident's dream of foreign invasion. I wonder if she is one of these Counterwhispering officers. They are certainly broader than most, and there *is* that little *plff, plff* sound that they make when they walk. I touch them. I show my identification card and I touch their snouts and their bellies. None of them is her. Nobody is her. I take down all the names and numbers of the highest officials in Counterwhispering. Nobody, none of them, is her. Then, convinced by the size of her body (as I remember it) that if she is not a high official, she must be really and truly diseased, I urgently request permission to visit the National Communal Prison.

"Long live our glorious Represident!" cries the officer as he hands me the authorization and the pass.

"Viva!" I officially repeat, and I touch his trunk.

No, he is not her either.

And now with the signed, sealed, and officially stamped authorization I make my way to the National Communal Prison.

19

FRAY BARTOLOMÉ DE LAS CASAS,

HIS ERROR

[Historia de Cuba, Vol. V]

It is a very dark not-night. Therefore from every direction, while the vermin on duty (twenty-four-hour shifts, with no days off) go about their jobs, one can hear them exclaiming the official words of praise for the not-night's amazing brightness. In the midst of this blinding brightness, I grope along until I bump into something soft, cold, skinny, and stinking—a female. My skin crawls at the contact with this creature. The bony, pestiferous beetle waves its claws around like a cockroach stranded on its back, but it does not move away from me. I push it and continue on my way. The whore emits a bleat or shriek or moan or whatever the fuck you call it, and I turn around. It stands there numbly, staring at me.

"Don't you remember me?" it says, and my fury grows, because I see that this is that same sweet-tongued insect that looked directly at me during the day, at the backside-swinging hour, when I was searching the crowd for my mother. The same gleaming eyes. The same plaintive, ingratiating look, like a kicked dog. No, I tell it, I don't remember a thing. But still she starts to come toward me, her claws outstretched and her bones clattering. I shove her away from me and I go on, looking for my mother.

20

VICTOR HUGO'S DREAM

[*Gaspard de la nuit*
Aloysius Bertrand]

Asshole.
Asshole.
Asshole.
Asshole.
Asshole.
And when I stop screaming this same word over and over (though I never for one instant stop walking and bumping into things and kicking), the not-night has ended. With the coming of the brightness of the grand-and-glorious-day there also bursts forth the thunderous anthem in praise of the Supreme Represident's kindness in granting us the infinite blessing of a new-and-glorious-day-of-joy. The *ga-ga-boom* of the period of mechanized labor begins, the bustling about increases, the hurrying and scurrying becomes dizzying, and the anthem is now at its grandest moment. The smelly ranks begin to close, and to hook into each other, and to form the not-buses. The cackling and gabbling grows louder and louder, the traffic snarls. The great army (multiple buses) of free children united by heavy hooks and chains marches off to its work areas intoning the prescribed hymns of praise. The women, bent so their knees and their heads are almost touching, transport great rocks, wield sledgehammers, and drag on cables as they glorify their liberation. And the men, those two-legged conglomerations of shit and slime—all they do, optimists that they are, is push and grunt and nod. There is the sound of cackling, heehawing, whinnying, several truncheon blows, and another whinny.

21

ON THE LABOR UNIONS OF TODAY

AND TROTSKY'S ERRORS

[Selected Works of V. I. Lenin]

The goose-stepping increases. The *crk-crk* of talons scraping across the ground raises clouds of dust. There is the thunderous sound of the Claws of Power whipping the backs of the Enemies of the Nation who are being marched toward their Appointment with Destiny. The cornet, or tin can, or horn, or whistle, or conch shell, or whatever the hell it is—what do I care, anyway—echoes, or sounds, or cries out, or calls, or shit, you get the picture. At the sound, there is a sudden and complete cessation of the terrible racket that the beasts have been making as they feverishly worked. The order has been given (with the cornet or flatulent flowerpot or how the hell am I supposed to know what it was) to stop working and to join the escort, goose-stepping and shrieking insulting slogans, that is driving the Enemies of the Nation, kicked and beaten, to their Appointment with Destiny, where they will be expunged from the rolls of the Mother-and-Fatherland.

The procession is formed in the following way: First, to the sound of the tambour or drum or hollow log or coffin lid or whatever the hell it is, come the High Dignitaries of the Land, the Chancellors and Vice-Chancellors, representatives of the High Secretary, and the delegations and post-delegations, accompanied by the Counterwhispering officers who supervised the trial and handed down the sentence. Behind them come immense signs, flags, pennants, and tatters of cloth and cardboard; at the midpoint of the procession, amidst artificial palm fronds and synthetic laurels, brass spears, fiery braziers, and loudspeaker-slogans, there is the State Palanquin, carried at a noble height, on which is borne the greater-than-life-size image of the Supreme Represident. Behind the gigantic image (which the entire crowd tries to bow down before and worship—an action prohibited by law and a prohibition enforced by kicks and truncheon blows from the elite Shock Troops), come the martial troops of the Counterwhispering Agents (Second Class). The troops are flanked by files of not-trucks filled with roaring rodents. After these troops comes the armed Corps of Counterwhisperers, carrying the implements of execution (wire, rocks, iron rods, sledgehammers, axes, rope, and the ever-present hooks, plus such outmoded and hard-to-find weapons as cannons, rifles, pistols, and machine guns).

Behind these—at the very end of the procession, in fact —come the screaming masses, with a regular, rhythmic, unanimous roar that grows softer, then louder, then softer, then louder, as the drum, or tom-tom, or bongo drum, or hollow log, or coffin lid, or whatever the hell it is, instructs them.

22

CAPITAL CHAPTER

[*El sisi*
Nicolás Tolentino]

The goose-stepping braying comes to a halt at the National Represidential Square. The bellowing mass of flesh is ordered, by the shaking of a wooden rattle, to stand within the area reserved for them. Those who are bearing the flaming torches and the image of our glorious Represident are ordered to stand within the area reserved for *them*. Those shouting and making noise go on shouting and making noise. The criminals about to be exterminated are herded into the area set aside for them. When these criminals pass by me, I take the opportunity offered me to show what I'm made of, and I kick the nearest one in the head several times (someone, even if I am unaware of it, is taking note of this, I know). The howling mass tries to imitate me. But agents from the Counterwhispering Corps step in. Those screaming go on screaming. Now the Enemies of the People are kneeling with their backs to us, in the officially prescribed position for receiving their well-deserved People's Justice. One of these criminals, a female, apparently stumbles as she falls to her knees, and she kicks the animal in front of her. That animal, a male, shoves the female that kicked him. At once there ensues a brief but furious struggle of kicks and bites among the victims who are about to be purified. The Counterwhispering troops immediately move in to pull them apart, and a few blows from the agents' Claws of Power pacify them.

Now the list of charges is produced, and an official standing beside the gigantic image of the Supreme Represent begins to read it. There is a litany of preliminary gobble-dygook that I confess I hardly pay attention to—*In witness of, whereby, thereby, subsequent to, concomitant upon, preconcomitant to, antepreconcomitant with, seeing that,* *under the conditions which, appearing upon, postsubse-quent to that prespecified in the appendix, in postdocu-ment such-and-such of postvolume so-and-so of the criminal code touching the testimony of the witness*—but then comes the part that matters: **WE FIND:** *that a terrible crime has been committed.* **The criminals are hereby charged as:** *Enemies of the People and of Its Infinite and Sole Leader.* **Sentence:** *Execution by Total Annihilation.* **Special circumstances:** *The condemned are granted the special favor of being executed by the Glorious Masses, represented by:* **first,** *the Special Agents of the Bureau of Counterwhispering;* **and then,** *the Glorious Masses them-selves.*

When the reading of the charges is ended, the cackling or drumming (or whatever the hell that noise was that ac-companied the reading) halts. This process is invariably somewhat long and ponderous, and parts of it even boring, but the next phase is much more interesting. With a club, the agents gauge the exact place on which the victim will be clubbed—always directly at the base of the skull. Then comes the "mock blow." The official who officiates over the clubbing (I have done this many times myself) raises the club, takes a deep breath, and lowers the club with fury, as though he were going to crush the condemned animal's skull. But just as the club is about to crash into the con-demned beast's brain, the officer stops in midair, and the club does not fall. This action, which is always accompa-nied by a howl of fury from the mock executioner, is re-peated three times. This act, which is meant to give a lesson to the masses, is also called the "symbolic club-bing." It is during these three symbolic blows with the club that the process is worth one's while, for it is highly instructive to see the face of the person who is about to be administered People's Justice. It is truly worth seeing the way the animal's eyes and mouth open, the faces the animal makes, when the club swishes through the air and then suddenly stops, and just barely brushes its skull. It is genuinely interesting, because even though the victim, who is expecting the fatal blow, fails to receive it, it cannot manage to grasp the fact that it did not, or to erase the impression that it *is* receiving it, and so there is time (since the condemned creature did *not* receive it) for it to express the stupor, the terror, and the pain which is the point of the exercise. That is why, when the Supreme Represident discovered this fascinating phenomenon, he ordered that the three symbolic blows become an official part of the ceremony. He wanted everyone to see the expression of horror on the face of the animal about to be purified. At the fourth blow (the only real one) there is no expression of horror. The club or cudgel or truncheon or Claw of Power or sledgehammer or belaying pin or old automobile steel spring or what the fuck difference does it make to *you* crashes down, and the animal's skull is instantly and fatally crushed. The impact is so great that the victim has no time to express pain or horror or any other emotion. With no further ado, and barely kicking, the animal simply crumples. . . . So the opportunity to see the expression of pain and horror and terror only arises during the three symbolic blows.

When the verminous beast dies, it falls forward, because the blow comes from behind. The spray of shit, bone, and blood is short and violent. As they kick, some of the animals' claws sometimes become tangled with others', so it is not easy to separate them. I have also seen some animals, in the middle of their *crk-splat* or kicking or bursting open or splashing or spraying or whatever the hell it is they do when they are bashed, claw at their eyes and pull them out of their heads; in other cases it is the club that pops their eyes out.

Now the masses leave the area that was assigned to them

and are herded into the execution area, where the victims with their skulls burst open are lying. To the sound of hymns and anthems, the masses, using tin cans, pieces of broken glass, or just their teeth and talons, rip them apart. This is the phase which can most strictly speaking be called the "People's Justice." I jump at once into the flock of crows and vultures and start, methodically and conscientiously, yet passionately, to join in. I throw myself onto the carpet of bodies lying there facedown, and I poke among them, searching. Like some madman in a wild search for justice, I kick through the bodies, turning them over, looking at their burst and broken faces, searching for that one face that interests me, and although I do not find it, I still go on hitting them, kicking at them, turning them over with the tip of my hind claws, examining them one by one. I wade through them violently, squashing them when I am done, looking at every one of them. At last my fury subsides, I grow calmer: none of them is my mother. She is not among these dead rats with broken necks and skulls. She still has not totally escaped me, I think. She is still mine, I can still be the one to exterminate her. And borne on a wave of euphoria, I make my way through the panting, puffing crowd praising the peerless goodness and unparalleled justice of the grand and glorious Supreme Represident. And since I am in such rare good humor (or at least not absolutely desperate, or utterly defeated, or whatever the fuck other depressive emotion I might be feeling but am not, goddammit), I utter a tiny whisper.

23

WHICH RECOUNTS THE FRIAR'S VISIT

TO THE GARDENS OF THE KING

[The Ill-Fated Peregrinations
of Fray Servando
Reinaldo Arenas]

Showing my card identifying me as a member of the Bureau of Counterwhispering, I at last receive authorization, and with it a permit (in the category *Admission Tolerated*), to inspect the immense National Communal Prison. I go inside, holding my identification card up in plain sight, as per regulations. The guards, with their faces so patently those of guards, watch my every movement, every step, as I advance through the enormous prison. There have been cases, though I do not remember them personally (and I am no youngster), in which the enemy, disguised as a friend (i.e., as a counterwhisperer), has gone through the checkpoint at the gate of the huge prison and attempted to remove a criminal just before the beast's Appointment with Destiny.

At the far end of the large open area I must walk through first, I come to the Containment Section. The location of each niche and nook along the long corridor that passes through this section is immediately distinguishable, for each one is lit by the shining of the prisoners' shaved heads. By order of our glorious Represident (a brilliant stroke), and with the unanimous support of the entire universe (including that part which is enemy territory), a decree was issued several years ago requiring that every prisoner be required to keep his head (shaved, of course) polished to a brilliant luster, to which end each prisoner was officially allotted a monthly quota of polish, with which he is required under the approving or reproving gaze of the appropriate Counterwhispering agent, to polish his head. The polish, acting upon the shaved skull, produces such a brilliant gleam that the condemned man, wherever he might be, "shines forth," and this means, obviously, that in case of attempted escape he can be instantly located and captured. And in order that his extermination may be quick and certain, all one has to do is shoot at the shine. This polish, also, thanks to the foresight of our brilliant Represident, was ordered to have phosphorescent qualities. Thus even during the not-night (which in some areas of the prison is perennial), the shaved heads of the prisoners, instead of not shining, shine all the more brightly. They sometimes even resemble lightning, or the Northern Lights. It has been said that the Supreme Represident, during his inspection visits to the National Communal Prisons (of which there are many, but they are all alike and so they all have the same name), derives immense pleasure from seeing through the darkness the luminous winking and twinkling of those craniums, which sometimes, losing control, whirl and flash about, crash into a wall, and burst. At those moments the trails of luminosity are so wonderful that one would think that we were celebrating our annual People's National Represiversary, and that those flashes and sparkles were rockets, glorious fireworks in homage to our immortal Represident.

Permit in hand, I walk on, constantly escorted by minor and major officials. I am at pains to recall that my official purpose (putative as it may be) is to review conditions in the enormous prison, and, with authorization from the Highest Authorities, to search for an alleged fugitive, or misplaced verminous number. Since everything is in order —I have the permit, the revenue stamps, and the official document stamped with the gold seal of the Supreme Represident and executed by his own High Secretary—I can come and go as I wish, into any cell, semi-cell, combo-cell, quasi-cell, not-cell, maxi-cell, or multi-cell I wish to.

In the multi-cells I must carefully inspect each and every

prisoner; there are many of them, and they are all sentenced to Total Annihilation. It is important to perform my first inspection here among those that will be undergoing Total Annihilation (a sentence issued directly from the Represidential Capital); it is very important that before I go into other areas of the prison I look carefully and closely at all these hideous faces I kick, all these shining skulls, all these stinking and hunchbacked masses of flesh that are about to be Totally Annihilated. The reason for this urgency is that a prisoner sentenced to Total Annihilation, once exterminated, will not exist—neither as a Post-Exterminated Prisoner, nor as an Exterminated Prisoner, nor as a Vile Traitor, nor as an Enemy of the People. He will simply not exist. Total Annihilation of a condemned prisoner requires the total annihilation of all members of the prisoner's family, all friends, acquaintances, and alleged friends and acquaintances, as well as all personal traces of the prisoner—all fingerprints, signatures, writings of any kind, etc., that the verminous creature may have left on this earth. Anyone who remembers the prisoner (and there are more than enough agents to search out those who might remember) will also be sentenced to Total Annihilation; anyone who wonders whether the prisoner ever existed also earns execution, and is forthwith executed. Even the prisoner's jailers, those who execute the prisoner, are sentenced to Total Annihilation—that is, they become Vermin by Association, and so, branded as rats (and regardless of the fact that they have been hand-picked to administer justice to the other vermin), they will be "justiced," as we sometimes call it, themselves.

Through the years this type of trial has become less and less complex. Most people, fearing that some acquaintance of theirs might one day be sentenced to Total Annihilation and therefore take with him anyone that knows him, now avoid any sort of relationship or acquaintance, any sort of friendship. Official orders and instructions (what we call *orientations*) also help in this process of disacquaintance.

Almost no one knows the person beside them at work—nor is anyone interested. In the Multi-Family everybody is on top of everybody else, but nobody knows anybody. They are *disacquainted*. No one has a name, and all orientations help to make sure that one stranger is exactly like every other stranger, so that no one can remember anybody in particular, and therefore no one can be remembered, and therefore even in the hypothetical case that one is told that somebody no longer exists (or never existed at all), nobody can prove the contrary, and in fact nobody even knows who they're talking about. The coupling of two vermin for purposes of procreation is carried out under review by, or the authority or permission or authorization of, Higher Authority, and therefore the two vermin that hook onto each other and beslime themselves actually have no reason to be acquainted with each other, and if they are, the consequences are on their own heads, and those consequences may be serious indeed. But generally speaking, today (and in the recent past) when two members of the community receive a Breeding Permit, they perform the procreative act as disacquaintances. The choice for the coupling (or "grappling," as it is sometimes also called) is made in the following way: One of the vermin points with his or her claw in one direction. If the other insect pointed to belongs to the opposite sex (which must be truthfully declared, because there is often no way to distinguish by simply looking), he or she raises his or her claw, and then, holding up the Breeding Permit so that it can be checked, the two animals wait until not-night and, virtually without seeing each other, perform the coupling. The mounting may also be performed during the day (always assuming that the properly signed and officially stamped permit is obtained), but however hard it may be for one person to remember another (save in exceptional cases), it is still prudent, in daytime couplings, to make absolutely sure of the disacquaintance by employing a breeding mask. When the act is finished, the two vermin return to their labors.

Another method employed in all hives (and naturally, then, in the Multi-Family) is that of constantly moving from one habitat to another, from one square yard to another, so that in this way mutual acquaintance may be avoided and mutual disacquaintance maintained. *Friendship* (a disgusting and counterproductive phenomenon, and a discarded word, both the phenomenon and the word now virtually unknown among the members of a hive or nest, and certainly of the Multi-Family) is one of the most frightening charges that can be leveled against a number. Everyone denies it, everyone knows how costly this imputation can prove to be. Recently there has been great progress in this area. Consciousness has been raised; disacquaintance of the Other—with the obvious exception of the agents of the Bureau of Counterwhispering—is virtually total. Who then is there that does not praise the genius and virtuosity of the Supreme Represident? In fact, any person that takes the time to study the Code of Total Annihilation in depth will be absolutely convinced of the brilliance and wisdom of our glorious Represident, for the practical effect of this law is that the Supreme Represident is granted total and absolute impunity. What can a Represident be accused of —which of course is a hypothetical question, unthinkable in real life—except of being a traitor? And what is the penalty for treason? Total Annihilation. And who shall be annihilated with the person sentenced to Total Annihilation? Everyone who knows the criminal. Thus, if the Supreme Represident were someday to be accused of treason and sentenced to Total Annihilation, the entire Universe would disappear. All glory to our sublime and glorious Represident! But to the ordinary run of slime in our Nation, the much feared sentence of Total Annihilation is often meted out. This category of execution requires many readjustments, adjustments, checks, and interpolations, however; it takes time. And thanks to the length of the process, I am able to scrutinize each and every one of these vermin before they will never have existed.

I go along then, aided by the agents and under-agents that are escorting me, examining and sometimes interrogating this repulsive, stinking mass of bodies. With my claw I raise heads, twist necks around, peer into orifices, looking for my mother, and since I do not find her, it is only logical that I should become enraged, and once in a while stomp this one or that one, punctuating the kick with a quotation from our Supreme Represent, to assure myself proper respect. To calm myself, or at least to conceal my fury somewhat, I ask, though I could not care less, about the charges against this or that disgusting criminal. But what need is there for charges against a cockroach? One simply stamps it out. . . .

This old man, for example, who is so weak he can hardly move his claws and who keeps making some sort of panting or puffing sound that seems to go from his asshole to his mouth and back again without ever exiting his body—what has he done? The agent, bringing his dewlaps close to my ear, whispers, half frightened, half mockingly, "The old man says, if you can believe it, that he remembers, or heard somebody say, that men once flew to the moon." I step back in shock, looking down at that creaking, stinking mass rocking back and forth, inflating and deflating. I pull my foot back, take good aim, and kick. Then I move on. . . .

"What about this one?" We are now in a not-cell, a space in the middle of a narrow corridor. "What did he do?" I ask, pointing at a boy squatting down with his head between his thighs, as though he were trying to smell his ass. "What's wrong with him?"

"You'll soon see for yourself, sir," the agent says to me, and giving the boy a hard kick in the back of the head, he orders the slimy creature to show his face. The mucus-covered insect, afraid of breaking the law even if an agent of the law orders him to break it, refuses to raise his head. The agent then stretches out his Claw of Power, hooks it to the slug's forehead, and pulls, showing me the creature's face. I see, almost with horror, two green eyes. "Enough," I say in disgust to the agent, who unhooks his Claw of

Power from the forehead of the boy, who immediately hides his head again.

We continue the inspection. Here, in the combo-cell, there are thousands of young men who "forgot" to cut their hair off to the roots. There, in mini-cells, there are people that got sick. This prisoner, shackled and kept behind thick bars, sighed one day. And in this not-cell, there is a woman shivering. The agent, without a word, goes over to her and hits her. Attracted by the officer's action, I go over and kick her a few times myself.

"What did she do?" I ask.

"She said, 'I'm cold,' " the officer explains to me. Infuriated, I attack her again. And we continue on, through infinite tunnels punctuated by phosphorescent slashes of light.

"If she had said '*It's* cold,' " the officer explains as we pass through the vault in which lie those who forgot the words or the tune as they intoned the prescribed anthems, "she might have been granted some mercy, but saying '*I'm* cold' . . . That *I'm* is totally unacceptable. . . . *I am*, asserting one's individuality that way . . ." He shakes his head.

As I listen to these arguments, which I know very well, we continue to walk past cells, semi-cells, combo-cells, not-cells, counter-cells, mini-cells, and quasi-cells. Our way lit by the brilliantly glowing head of a prisoner-guide, we descend into the National Communal Sewers. In the Total Annihilation Execution Cell Ante-Chamber, constantly illuminated by the heads of the prisoners of the day, the last Confession Treatment is being given to a prisoner. A man? A woman? I am not certain. You cannot tell by looking. As a moment's logical reflection will show, by the time a prisoner arrives at this chamber in the Hall of Retractations, he (or she, or let us say "it," out of respect for the total ambiguity of the situation) has already lost every sign or mark that might distinguish between a man, a woman, and a dog. Without fingernails, or eyes, or hair, or sexual organs, or skin, who on earth can tell the difference between a large rat and a girl and a woman, or between a boy and a pig?

The unidentifiable mass vibrates gently each time the Confession Treatment is applied to it. But it continues to refuse to sign the confession that has been written out for it. I stand there for a few moments watching. The long rod probes all the mass's orifices, pokes around, jumps, looks for a place where the thing still has some feeling, and then digs in. At once a second confessor pours on the boiling liquid metal, the thing vibrates a little again, the rod penetrates the mass, but the stump of the claw still refuses to scribble its name on the neatly typewritten confession.

Curious, I ask what it is the criminal is refusing to talk about.

"It's not that it's refusing to talk," one of the confessors tells me as he prepares another rod. "It's that it's talking too much—and it's telling lies. It told us it heard somebody say that someplace there existed a list or roll or something where the names of the Represidential Capital, the various Servo-Perimeters, and the Satellite Cities were written, and even the names of our glorious Represident and all the rest of us, even the name of this animal getting the Confession Treatment," and here he prods the slug with the rod again, "and it says it also heard somebody say that when all this disappears, that list or roll or whatever it is will still be there, and because of it, everything that we—by order of the Supreme Represident, of course, I mean to say—that we struggle so hard to wipe out will be discovered. The only thing that we're asking of this animal before it's Totally Annihilated," and here he plunges the rod again into the mass where the beast's eyes once were, "is that it deny what it says it heard and that it sign the confession. We've tried to explain"—burying the rod in flesh—"that even if that list or whatever it is existed, once it was burned up it wouldn't exist anymore, and therefore this criminal would be exposed as a liar and a charlatan," and the confessor buries the rod with fury.

"But what does it say to that?" I ask.

"What does it say?" the Head Confessor says sternly, pouring the boiling liquid metal onto the peeled body, which bubbles and emits faint *glug-glugs*. "It says that even if that list were to be found, nobody would ever find the other one, which has the same information on it."

"So why don't you just finish the animal off?" I ask angrily, so angrily in fact that, unable to restrain myself, I pick up a rod and plunge it into the mass myself. Now the mass does not even quiver.

"The Supreme Represent," the confessor confesses to me in a low voice, "doesn't want it annihilated until we extract a claw-written signature on the Confession Certificate that everything it's said is false, and especially the part about those lists. Nobody's ever been able to find them, though we've turned the country upside down looking. If this goes on much longer," the confessor tells me in a worried tone of voice, "the word is that the palpably glorious Supreme Represent in person will come down here and try to obtain the denial-slash-confession with his own hands."

"Tell me," I say to the Head Confessor, stepping a step nearer that pestiferous, soughing mass writhing gently on the ground, "was it a man or a woman?"

"He was a traitor," he rebukes me furiously, and turning, he plunges the rod into one of the few sensitive spots still left.

Assured that the verminous creature had been male, and not my mother, I take a few notes and then, bored by the pointlessness of the interrogation, I continue my inspection.

A sea of shaved heads, more phosphorescence, the same sickening criminals with their repetitious crimes: people that forgot to raise their hands in an assembly, people that forgot the words to an anthem, people that consciously or unconsciously whispered, or who failed to denounce someone that supposedly whispered, women who without the authorized pass pissed, young people that forgot to shave their heads for one day, entire armies that forgot the password, or the correct words to the particular day's cheers. Plotters and schemers against history, monsters that wanted to poison our future by talking about mysterious and nonexistent lists in which all of our names appear, even if we no longer are alive, even if we have been sentenced to Total Annihilation. Traitors that did not have the patriotic balls to gouge out their eyes when they realized that they were green or blue instead of iron-colored, to match our heroic people's. Vermin with straight noses and small ears, and even hands instead of claws, who also did not have the patriotic courage to weed out all those signs of decadence and of the remote and miserable past, which is never coming back. And even that raving madman talking about a voyage to the moon. . . .

Immense cells lit by the phosphorescent heads of those who, having received a Breeding Permit, did not perform the coupling correctly, or, more serious yet, interrupted or aborted the growth of the population of the great communal republic, or, most serious of all, used their permission, and the free time granted them for the mounting, fruitlessly— that is, with treasonous intent. Criminals, in a word—horrible and nauseating vermin. I still can remember one of them, a woman, who said that she had composed a samphony, or symphony, or saxophony, or some other idiotic word I certainly have no reason to remember, using whistles, drums, trumpets, hollow logs, tom-toms, and how the hell do I know what else, and even that she asked permission to play it. . . . Drunkards, swine, dogs, horrible rats, *BEASTS*, and they will all be Totally Annihilated at any moment, as they deserve. I have inspected every one of them, kicked and insulted every one of them, or simply erased them with a meta-report. I have observed them. But my mother is not among them, among these vermin that now (because it is now not-night) are arguing and fighting with their claws and talons among themselves in their cells, semi-cells, combo-cells, not-cells, quasi-cells, maxi-cells, mini-cells, and counter-cells, emitting their pathetic and maddened phosphorescence. My mother is not there. No, not here. With my claw I scribble my report in the inspection log. *Long live our glorious Represident!* I cry. And I move on.

REINALDO ARENAS

24

THE VISION OF ANAHUAC

[*Antologia*
Alfonso Reyes]

OFFICIAL FINDINGS

1. If the female accused by the Nation had at least not said anything while she was shivering, even though shivering is itself an act of criminal deviance, contrary to the maintenance of public order, and *prima facie* evidence of decadence, then the above-mentioned Enemy of the People (argued her Attorneys-at-Extenuation) would only have been sentenced to Simple Extermination.

2. If the female accused by the Nation had, upon shivering, even though shivering is itself an act of criminal deviance, [etc.], said "*It is* cold," instead of what she did say, then the use of that phrase "*It is*," in an impersonal manner, would have operated as a counter-aggravating circumstance, and therefore she would only have been tried and found guilty and sentenced to Compound Extermination, i.e., Confession Treatment and Decapitation.

3. If the female accused by the Nation had said, "*We are* cold," instead of "*I am* cold," it would have lain within the power of the honorable and impartial members of the Commission on Extenuation to have entertained the argument, in sympathy with the accused, that she was expressing, communally, a collective idea, and therefore she would only have been required to perform an Act of Public Retractation and a Pre-Decapitation Exhibition in a refrigerator car, in which she would constantly have been required to exclaim *How hot it is! How hot it is!*, followed by Decapitation.

4. The female accused by the Nation, however, in employing the phrase *"I am,"* clearly expressed her state of aberrant and deviant individual criminality; she declared herself an irreconcilable enemy of the national communal philosophy, and therefore of the Nation itself, and therefore of our glorious Represident. The use of this phrase (*"I am"*) confirms that she is an agent of the enemy, a confusionist diversionist deviationist, and reveals her to us in all her criminal depravity. She is an individualist with ideas of her own regarding temperature and her egoistic personhood, and furthermore commits the barbarous and arrogant error of confessing that fact publicly.

For all these reasons, we therefore and hereby unanimously **FIND** and **DECREE** the following **VERDICT:**

That this verminous creature be subjected to the Maximum Punishment, Total Annihilation, with all the ceremonies, retractations, rectifications, and counter-rectifications thereunto pertaining. This punishment shall also be meted out to all the guilty party's family members, acquaintances, quasi-acquaintances, near-acquaintances, and those mentioned or alluded to by her in any regard whatsoever. And to that effect, we sign and affix our seal hereto, under the glorious image of our glorious Prime Mover, the Represident of the Nation.

> [*Here the document displays the Seal of the Nation, superimposed upon the signatures of the members of the People's Tribunal of Destiny.*]

25

CONCERNING THOSE THINGS

THAT OCCURRED IN SEVILLE UP UNTIL

HIS EMBARKATION FOR THE INDIES

[Historia de la vida del
Buscón llamado Don Pablos
Francisco de Quevedo]

I left that Servo-Perimeter and came to another. I was subjected to the same procedures for visiting the National Communal Prison in this sector.

Sometimes in this particular prison the prisoners do hard labor related to the crime they committed. The basic work of this zone, for example, is singing anthems in praise of the Supreme Represident, and there is a Perimeter Choral Corps constituted for that purpose. Most of the members of this perimeter-chorus who have been sentenced to Total Annihilation were originally accused of the crime of Illegal Possession of Tin Ears. I walk on, and finally I come to a Satellite City checkpoint. I go through, holding my membership card aloft as required. My search is most efficient; I myself execute a few of the guilty citizens I discover. This morning, in fact, to great fanfare (and other concomitant accoutrements), I have been called to the Satellite City regiment headquarters.

Trumpets sound. The Counterwhispering officer-in-charge is standing at the entrance, flanked by his battalion, which gives three howls in my honor. Now the officer, carrying a large iron box, steps up to me. *Worthy agent of the immortal Nation and of our glorious Supreme Repres-*

ident, he says, *in recognition of your untiring efforts and supremely efficient labor against the Enemies of our People, it is our great honor to bestow upon you, by personal order of the High Secretary, the Order of National Patriotism, Third Degree.* Huzzahs and trumpets sound again. The troops once more howl in my honor. I make the prescribed salute of unworthy gratitude and I inspect all the personnel that surround me, including the officer putting the sash on me. *She won't hide under these helmets, the miserable bitch,* I think. Though enraged, I put my words of thanks in order and I say:

> Long live our glorious Represident! I shall never yield in my battle against the enemy, not for a single second. The honor of this sash will spur me on to ever higher goals, to ever greater achievements, and to ever more effective performance of my duty. Long live our glorious Supreme Represident!

The horns bleat another fanfare. I inspect the horn players. She is not among them, she is not here. Quickly I make my way over to the Executive Offices of the Zonal Branch of the Bureau of Counterwhispering. The agents salute when they see me.

"I want," I say, "to carry out a complete inspection of all Counterwhispering agents and all inmates of the Concentrated Rehabilitation Camp."

"Your first request," the Counterwhispering zonal chief has the nerve to say, "involves state secrets. You must have permission from the Office of the Represident."

I show him my scroll and my sash, and then I pull out the authorization which gives me explicit permission to inspect all Counterwhispering files and all files on all criminals. At the same time, I send the officer who had dared stand in my way to prison. Charge: Obstruction of Patriotic Procedures. Crime: Enemy of the People. Sentence: Total Annihilation.

Now I sit in rage and fury before the files being brought to me day and not-night in not-trucks, and with painstaking patience, one by one, I review the faces of every agent of the Bureau of Counterwhispering.

26

LETTER FROM JOSÉ MARTÍ

TO THE ARGENTINE AMBASSADOR

[Complete Works of José Martí]

Exhausted after having pored through most of the Counter-whispering Headquarter's agent files, which now lie in piles across the width and breadth of this Satellite City, I go out for a walk. The streets, as in all Satellite Cities, are laid out in narrow rectangles separating one Counterwhispering block office from another, one Communal Police Precinct from another, one Multi-Family from another. Every ten blocks, there is a not-park with its standard not-benches, hooks, and Cells on Wheels. Seldom does anything happen in a Satellite City. At the given hour, everyone falls down; at the given hour, everyone gets up again. And at the given hour everyone makes the regulation sound. There is great fanaticism for the Represident in these cities; even the people at liberty go beyond the call of duty with regard to head-shaving and the like, and by far the great majority of them voluntarily apply the skull polish to their heads so that they can more readily be identified. The voluntary use of the polish among free men has become so general, in fact, that anyone who does not use it is almost openly considered an Enemy of the People and can easily find that he is the re-cipient of People's Justice. If such were not the case, why would almost all the skulls, both large and small, be pol-ished to a high shine the way they are? And there is yet another remarkable consequence of our glorious Represi-dent's brilliant ideas that one can observe here, for lacking

REINALDO ARENAS

as the Satellite Cities do many of the advantages of the Represidential Capital, and possessing no light but that available at the checkpoints and in the offices of the Bureau of Counterwhispering, many of them have found that the skull polish compensates for the lack of more standard illumination during the not-nights.

I continue walking, following the winking of those skulls. Sometimes, when a particular head does not glow sufficiently, I shut the animal up in the nearest Cell on Wheels. It is the obligation of all citizens that when a criminal is captured and led to the Cell on Wheels, everyone must begin to sing an anthem to the Supreme Represident, employing, of course, the hymns and praises specified by the regulation anthem-book.

The criminal I have captured, whose shaved head did not shine brightly enough, begins singing at the top of his lungs.

"That'll get you nowhere, you son of a bitch," I tell him, irritated by all the racket, and I make a note beside his name: *Suspected whisperer.* The accused, now locked up and booked, looks down at the charge branded on his chest and, not looking at me, as regulations prescribe, begins again to sing, over and over again, and now even more impassionedly, the anthems to our glorious Represident and the justice of the Nation.

Long live our glorious Represident! he cries when I turn away.

I go back to him, and with the branding iron for branding the charges on criminals I brand another charge on his chest: *Public whisperer. Sentence: Total Annihilation.* The criminal deviant looks down at the sentence and sings another hymn of praise. *That's always the way with this scum,* I think. *Even when the rod goes through their throat and they spew out shit and guts and blood, they keep singing hymns to the Supreme Represident. That's the way they are.*

27

CLOCKS AND STEAM ENGINES

[Claude Lévi-Strauss]

So I continue on, until I stumble on a lump, one of the members of this Satellite City community. When I feel myself in contact with that cold, milky-white, bony, stinking, half-moon-shaped thing that I realize is a human being, I stagger backward and I vomit. Instead of running away, however, the thing slinks closer to me, while I am still vomiting up everything I have eaten in this Perimeter. Unable to contain my fury, I hold the animal down with my claw. Now the clucking thing dares to speak to me.

"Don't you remember me?"

I recognize the creature; this is the cow-eyed female that invited me to swing my backside with her, the female I ran into back there somewhere, I think in the first Servo-Perimeter. While it is unheard-of for her to dare touch me and speak to me, it is even more outrageous that she should use the word *remember*. We all know that many people have been sentenced to Total Annihilation for using that word. Intrigued by a person so imbecilic—or perhaps so utterly evil—I make an effort to control my rage. She might be a Counterwhispering agent sent to test me.

"Uh-huh," I say, "I remember."

"Back there," she says.

"Uh-huh," I say.

"In the Servo-Perimeter," she says.

"The first Servo-Perimeter," I say.

"Uh-huh," she says.

"What do you do?" I ask her.

"I do what everybody does," she answers.

"Everyone's job in this Satellite City is to manufacture the glorious badges and banners," I say.

"Uh-huh," she says. "Everyone does that."

"But what are you doing *now*, since you're not manufacturing badges?" I ask.

"I'm on my authorized energy-recuperation period," she says.

"We could walk a little," I say.

"I'm authorized," she says.

"To use the word *remember*, too?" I ask.

"The use of that word is not absolutely prohibited," she replies.

"So you know what it might cost you," I say.

"If somebody besides you should hear me say it, uh-huh," she replies.

"Do you know who I am?" I ask her.

"I saw you," she says, "when you were inspecting the camp."

"And?" I say.

"You looked at me, too," she says.

"What is it you want?" I ask her.

"I mean, we looked at each other," she says.

"So?" I say.

"Two people hardly ever look at each other in the community," she says.

"Is that right?" I say.

"You dared to look at me . . ." she says.

"Uh-huh," I say.

"People may bump into each other, but they don't look at each other," she says. "And we looked into each other's eyes," she says. "When we looked at each other we looked at each other . . ."

And she goes on talking that way, saying that if when I looked at her she looked back then we looked at each other and if we looked at each other then I looked at her when she looked at me, and that if when she looked at me

I kept looking at her, well then . . . And gradually the rage that has been building in me for this teary-eyed cow grows, and grows, and grows, and now the whore is actually beginning to insinuate personal motives, and still she goes on talking: *Because if you looked at me when I looked at you, and you kept looking at me even when I looked back at you . . .*

"What is it you want?" I finally interrupt, seizing her by the throat with my Claw of Power.

"What I want, what I want . . ." she says, but then she stops babbling, the filthy rodent, without ever saying what the fuck it is she wants. "When you looked at me, when you looked . . ." is all she says.

Enraged, I drop her, and although I still think she may be an investigator from the Bureau, or an *agent provocateur,* the disgust and revulsion I feel for her at this moment is so great that I can hardly restrain myself. The fact that her authorized energy-recuperation period has not yet expired makes me suspicious. No one dares just stroll around like this, take a walk, have a conversation, without a pass, I think. But for tactical reasons I do not ask to see this female's pass, I simply continue to walk along beside her.

"Have you received orientations to go someplace?" I ask her.

"What?" she says.

"Are you oriented to go someplace in particular at this moment?" I repeat.

At that, she begins to speak, or rather to stammer—"Oriented, oriented . . . no," she says. "Disoriented, disoriented, disoriented . . ."

"What are you saying?!" I shout, but then I control myself. She is obviously an agent, I think, and I keep walking.

"Disoriented, disoriented," she is saying now, more spiritedly, or rather the spiritedness extends into the middle of the word, but then it falls, so she is speaking like this: "*Disorien*-ted, *disorien*-ted, -ted, -ted . . . Let's go," the disgusting sow finally says, as she takes one of my claws between her own. I am about to burst with rage.

REINALDO ARENAS

"Do you have some extrazonal place?" I ask, pretending to go along with her.

She looks at me even more directly, and with eyes even brighter, and squeezing my claw, she pulls me, and says to follow her.

The place is constructed out of two placards and a smooth rock; on the ground there is some dry material, a material like straw or claw clippings. She lies down on it.

"*Disorien*-ted, *disoriennnnnnn*-ted," she sings, and she beckons to me with her eyes. I remain standing over her, looking at her.

"What are we doing here?" I ask. "Why do you have this place?"

She does not say a word. She sits up in the straw or claw parings, picks up some sort of stick or something, and begins to breathe deeply—she is panting, puffing, and making a terrible noise.

"Do you like my place?" she asks me.

I go on looking down at her, without replying. This seems to excite her even more, because her snorting increases.

"Sit down here, beside me," she says. But I remain standing. Then, still making that horrible noise, now with her entire body, she crawls toward me, almost on her knees. Standing there, I look down at her: there she is, while from her eyes there come two drops of water.

"What's wrong?" I say.

"*Disorien*-ted, *disorien*-ted . . ." she says, and throwing down the stick or whatever it was she was holding, she stretches one of her claws out toward me. The claw trembles; finally it touches me, at the waist.

"I'm disoriented," she says. "You seem different . . ." And her claw is still touching my waist.

"What does that mean?" I ask. But she doesn't answer me. Her panting intensifies, her shaved head rises and falls with her breathing, then starts bobbing faster and faster, and finally it falls forward. Her forehead is now lying on my multi-overalls, between my legs. Then, moaning, she raises her head and begins to touch me with her lips. My flesh crawls, but I control myself. I must prove to her, if she is an agent, that she will get nothing out of me, that she will never succeed in what she is attempting to do, that my patriotic will, my determination, and my sense of duty are stronger than all ruse and temptation. The whore-agent is very skillful; she squeezes and moans, and at last manages to introduce one of her claws into my multi-overalls. At that, I can no longer control my repugnance, and deciding moreover that enough is enough, that I have shown that I am infallible, and that therefore she can now identify herself and grant me the Order of Unshakable Purity, I step back. But as though her duty were not yet done, she twines herself around my legs and continues to caress me.

"You have done your duty well, as I have done mine," I say. "We can identify ourselves to each other now. You cannot refuse to grant me the order . . ."

"What?" she says.

"We can identify ourselves now," I say. And I pull out my membership card so that she can make her check mark on the list of temptations avoided.

"That's not . . ." she says. "I don't have anything to do with any of that. You're mistaken. I, I just wanted to share . . ."

"What?" I say. "What are you saying?"

"I . . . am . . . *disorien*-ted," she says, still on her knees, and still pawing me.

Little by little, I feel a terrible rage coming over me. So I have been pawed by the enemy, by the worst of enemies, as our glorious Represident declared in one speech, because this is evil, a sickness, a criminal who preys on others and who employs any subterfuge or demonic cunning to do so. And so, still remembering our glorious Represident's speech, livid with fury, I take the creature by her ears, I lift her off the ground, I drop her, and then I lift her up again.

"*Disorien*-ted, *disorien*-ted," the criminal goes on muttering. And she looks at me with those big mare's eyes of hers.

"What did you say?" I say now, about to crush her.

"I said I'm all alone, I need you . . ."

And when I hear these words, my rage explodes, and I can no longer control myself. I am boiling with fury, my face writhes, my claws slither toward her throat. Trembling with fury and revulsion, I seize her, and whatever it was that she was going to say sticks in her filthy throat, her immense eyes turn redder and redder until they turn black, and at last, bursting, they pop out of her skull, bathing my official multi-overalls in blood. Even more nauseated by the female's blood, I throw her lifeless body to the ground and kick it over and over again; I scrawl on it the mark of Enemy First Class: Fundamental Enemy. With one blow I stamp my number on it. And I begin to run through the Satellite City. I run, but I cannot subdue or control my rage; I run, hitting myself with my own Claw of Power and howling in rage and fury and hatred against myself. *She touched me, the filthy creature touched me, I have been pawed by that disgusting rodent.* I shiver in disgust, and I go on beating myself. *She touched me, she squeezed me.* As I run, I vomit. My flesh crawls.

28

PROLOGUE AND EPILOGUE

[*The Palace of the White Skunks*
Reinaldo Arenas]

When the cockroach tries to run, it crawls up and down, slithers this way and that way, all over the place. If it runs this way, the people here squash it, *splat*; if it runs that way, the people over that way squash it. If it crawls up—*splat*. If it crawls down—*splat*. There is no escape. Once a year, as we approach the anniversary of the Triumph of Our Glorious Supreme Represident, all citizens of the Nation are authorized by order of the Represident himself to kill cockroaches. The rest of the year, killing those insects—as well as any other kind of pest or vermin—is, except in exceptional cases, prohibited. Not for protection of the species, but because of the redirection (loss) of productive strength and effort which this action entails.

Nonetheless, today is the day. The Represiversary approaches, and our wise and glorious Represident (eternal honor to him), in recognition of the violent criminal instincts natural to every human being, has offered us the opportunity to discharge some of those energies. . . .

The six-legged creature scurries about, and the larger, two-legged creatures pursue it. The cockroach, doomed, lies belly up. That is the moment to observe the face of the common citizen of our Nation, instants before squashing the cockroach. The eyes sparkle with delight, the lips drool, there is a smile.

The celebration is universal, the fury with which every citizen ferrets out the cockroach and pursues it is epic and unanimous. What a revelry of hate. And what perfect co-ordination. The noise of the beaters is directed with con-summate skill. This is the day—in the Represidential Capital, the Servo-Perimeters and Satellite Cities, and every other inhabited place in the Nation—of the Cockroach Ex-termination. What cheers and shouting. Even those who have been sentenced to Total Annihilation are allowed to take part in this grand, worldwide ceremony. What a racket. Everyone kills cockroaches.

In the Concentrated Rehabilitation Camps, the rod, the juicer, the pick, the shovel, and the spitting have been called off today, and all one can hear is the *splat-splat-splat* of the squashing of cockroaches. In the great Halls of Re-tractation, in the cells, quasi-cells, mini-cells, maxi-cells, and not-cells of the Communal Prisons, the machinery of imprisonment—the neckrings, the probes, the liquid metal, the Claws of Power, the eyepullers, the anti-testicular de-vices and the tripe-extracting machines, the nail-strippers, and the foot-reducers, among other pieces of apparatus—lie untouched, the patriotic tasks to which they are dedicated postponed until tomorrow, and amidst the wild phospho-rescent winking of countless shaved skulls all one can hear is the *squish-squish-squish* of the prisoners' suppurating feet and the *splat-splat-splat* of the cockroaches as the pris-oners, even as they are condemned to death, carry out ex-ecutions of their own.

Splat! Splat! What a noise. Even the agents in charge of the represidential loudspeakers leave their posts—the re-presidential hymns are not sung today—and join the na-tional massacre. The combat grows fiercer, the battle is joined, and in the heat of the fight, disputes over the *coup de grace* of a cockroach are not unknown, for while there are more than enough insects to go around during the first hours of the day, as the hours wear on there are fewer and fewer. It becomes rarer and rarer to see a cockroach lurking in a corner, or in the fold of a wrinkled poster; it is impos-sible to find one running in the open. Now, therefore, it is not the killing of the cockroaches that spurs on the masses, it is the pursuit and capture of them.

And this second phase is even more exciting than the first. Entire platoons of rabid citizens dig into one small hiding place. If they chance to find a cockroach, what a scuffle ensues. I have seen two or three citizens claw out each other's eyes over a kicking cockroach, arguing over who will be the one to squash it. The platoons split up— some go this way, some go that. Leaving no stone unturned, the eager troops leap, run, poke about, crawl, sweep the ground with their eyes, investigate every nook, hole, or cranny with their claws, their very tongues.

With the first shadows of not-night comes an ever increasing bustle—*Hurry, we've got to hurry.* The *splat-splat-splat* of millions and millions of (larger) citizens sending millions and millions more (smaller) verminous creatures to their doom becomes deafening. (This pursuit and extermination, as our glorious Represident foresaw, enables the citizens of our Nation to forget for a time that they themselves are vermin, or for some, to take revenge on others because they know they are, and for almost all, to simply work off their violent instincts in socially acceptable ways.) From my Counterwhispering watchtower, I too squash not a few insects—not because I have any real interest in killing cockroaches, but because of the look the Counterwhispering agent in the other tower gives me (when I am not looking, of course). *Splat,* I go, and I look down at the shrieking masses below, violent, burning with true and sincere patriotic zeal. I see them sniff out cockroaches, drag cockroaches out of hiding; I see how they howl when they have one cornered, how when they almost miraculously ferret one out they throw themselves on it like a pack of wild dogs, disputing among themselves with teeth and claws for the honor (and blood) of the kill. *At this moment, this same spectacle is occurring in every corner of the free universe,* I think. And noting that the other agent is not looking my way, I laugh.

29

TO THE STARS

[*Selected Poems*
Fray Luis de León]

Since my mother, then—the rotten whore—is not over that way, or this way, or down here, or behind bars in the Communal Prisons, I go out into the fields of the Concentrated Rehabilitation Farm Camp. Because of the system employed for regulating the work in these fields, the review and inspection of those sentenced to the camps is easy.

The fields are great flat expanses of scorched earth. The scorching of the fields, although it has been done on purpose, is officially claimed to have been caused by the Great Patriotic War. Each inmate's work is defined as "making the desert less arid." And since there is no irrigation of any kind, natural or artificial, in these fields, the only method of accomplishing that task is "human irrigation," which is performed in the following way: At each end of the field there is a long metal bar, which is entrusted to the hands of (or supervised by) special agents. The Rehabilitation Camp inmates (fitted, logically enough, with a large ring around their necks) file up to one end of the bar, and they are threaded onto it by their rings. Once that bar is full, another group of inmates picks it up at each end. These are the inmates that move the bar along, and they are not required to spit; the spitting is done by the others, those inmates skewered onto the bar by their rings. That in fact is their work: to walk along spitting time after time after time onto the flat expanse of the field, in order to impart to it some humidity. Once the bar has reached the other end of the field, the return begins—backwards, naturally, since it is impossible to turn around with a rigid bar of that length to which are attached as many as a thousand inmates by the rings around their necks. So backwards they march, the thousand inmates, spitting as they go, until they have reached the place they started from, at the other end of the field. Although, as I just explained, the inmates guiding the bar along are not absolutely required to spit, they sometimes do—perhaps as a means of encouraging and inspiring the spitters, although that is really not necessary since the agents, stationed on each hillock along the plowed field, keep a keen eye on the march of the spitters, and (well trained at this) they can detect on the instant if an inmate has ducked his head along with the rest but has failed to spit. In that case, rare though it may be, the agent whistles, and the progress of the bar, or the skewer, or the shish kebab, or the rod, or whatever the hell you call it, stops. The non-spitter is automatically taken out of his neckring and led off, without a question or a word, to the water tower that stands at the edge of the field. No one sees the non-spitter climb the little stairs up to the top of the water tower, because all inmates must continue to duck their heads at regular intervals and spit, but I can report that the process followed with the non-spitter is as follows: When the non-spitter has climbed the stairs to the top, he is led along a catwalk to the lip of the tank, and the agent, with a quick movement, pushes the lawbreaker over the edge. The weight of the inmate falling into the tank sets in motion its toothed arms and pulleys, and the criminal is pulped. The juice that the mill extracts from the non-spitter runs down a pipe into an irrigation ditch, and from the ditch it is absorbed into the thirsty earth. The non-liquid portion of the non-spitter (although there is very little of it) is sent to the compost heap beneath, and transformed into fertilizer. Although my purpose is to discover whether my mother is among these prisoners, it is essential that I constantly keep an eye on the water tower, in case without my noticing, the woman I am tracking down so that I can annihilate her should run between my legs as patriotic irrigation, moistening my official multi-overalls. And the rest of my life should become one long fruitless search. So while I officially review, inspect, and kick, I never take my eyes off that steep little ladder that leads up to the tank on the top of the Rehabilitation Camp water tower.

30

CLODIO GIUETH HIS LETTER TO AURIƒTELA;

THE BARBARIAN ANTHONY

KILLETH HIM BY MIƒCHANCE

[*The Travels of Persiles and Sigismunda*
Miguel de Cervantes]

Do you suppose she knows that I am looking for her? How long do you suppose she may have known? I have a feeling a good while. Maybe even since before I knew myself that I had to try to find her, find her and kill her. She knows a lot. When she used to look at me, and I remember this as though it were yesterday, she was not looking at me just to look at me, the way I am told mothers look at you; she was looking at me to see what new weakness she could discover in me, what flaw she could detect, what mistake she could scold me for. When she would talk to me, behind what she was saying there was something else. It was difficult to criticize or fault her for it, or make her admit it, because she would not actually *say* anything, but there would be a message of insult and humiliation that she was sending—and that I alone could receive. So I could never lay any blame on her for it, or complain, or prove it, since the message was meant for me alone, and I was the only one that caught it. You should have seen her face when she looked at me—it might be at the table, or in the living room, or at the door as I was leaving for work. It was a smirk, a look of mockery. Not open mockery, never an open smirk, because everything about her was cloaked in a

REINALDO ARENAS

pose of shyness, of fear, of tentativeness, as though she were afraid of me. "Criminal," she would have screamed at me, if I had so much as raised my voice to her. If you had looked closely, though, if you had looked underneath that apparent clumsiness she put on, as though she were some scared little mouse . . . Her mechanisms were (are) fearsome, and as vast as imbecility. She uses everything, and she uses everything to great advantage: love, weeping, whining, laughter, sickness, singing, hatred, tenderness, and above all that typical, diabolical, devastating, humiliating, unbearable, sly, hateful, crushing way of hers of saying Son . . . to me.

A whistle—no doubt because someone failed to spit. Sure enough, someone is now climbing the stairs up to the immense tank on top of the water tower. I run over, rush up the stairs, and position myself directly behind the escort of guards. Now I am on the catwalk that circles the tank. I see the non-spitter's back as he (or she) marches toward the juicing mechanism. I take out my documents and my counter-whistle, and I blow it. The agent turns around, the non-spitter stops. His (or her) back is still turned to me.

"I demand to inspect the prisoner before juicing," I say.

The prisoner, back turned to me, seems to shudder when he (or she) hears my voice, although it may not have been my voice that made him (or her) shudder, but rather the word juicing. The agent, as imbecilic as all the officials in the farm camps, barely understands me. I realize he can barely speak the language; as for the written word, the only thing he can decipher on my authorization is the letters that spell out "representional." So I decide to try to gain some time, and I step forward toward the prisoner about to be juiced so that I can see his (or her) face. But the idiotic animal of a guard, stepping between me and the condemned prisoner (now standing on the very verge of Patriotic Extraction), touches me. When I feel the claw of the agent touch me, I am so nauseated that I cannot bear it, and I howl as I push him into the tank. The juicing mechanism knows no distinctions—the stinking, reeking mass is transformed, in moments, into patriotic irrigation. When the other reptile, which had been stunned into stupefaction by the imminent carrying-out of its sentence, sees the effect of the juicing on the ex-agent, it leaps over the top of the water tank and out into the field on the other side, runs across the no-man's-land and zigzags through the watchtowers and the lines of prisoners skewered to their rods. The towers and the prisoners block the escaping prisoner from my sight.

"That has to be my mother," I think, "it has to be my mother. I'll be the one to liquidate her."

And leaping over platoons of spitted and spitting prisoners, running across the fields planted with watchtowers, I am off like a shot after that dodging, running body.

31

ASSEMBLY FOR GATHERING OF WITHES

TO BE USED IN TOBACCO DRYING,

IN PINAR DEL RIO

[*Juventud Rebelde* newspaper]

Inspired by my rage, I instruct the checkpoints and lookout towers and the rest of the pursuit personnel not to move; I tell them that I am taking upon my own patriotic shoulders the entire responsibility for the escaping prisoner's capture.

"It is the only way," I tell them, "to correct my error." Meantime, I am thinking *It's the only way for* me (*and not somebody else*) *to kill that creature that could so easily be her.* And I run, spurred on by my hate.

32

FORTUNE VISITS US

IN SPITE OF THE RAIN

[Mi tío el empleado
Ramón Meza]

The inmate, crossing the first rows of fields, has now gained the second rows. The Counterwhispering agents stand expectantly, waiting to see what action I take. If I fail, if the prisoner escapes (which is impossible), they will be the first to point the finger at me, as it is their patriotic duty to do, and I will be tried, as the situation demands, for complicity. The prisoner keeps going, now into the next rows of fields. *Where does that animal get the energy to run like that?* I wonder. I move a little faster. Now the verminous creature, finally tiring, is crawling along on all fours, although it is still moving at a considerable clip. The rodent slips between the claws of the other beasts, who go on marching impassively, spitting, irrigating, under the overseeing eye of an agent. The reptile's speed meanwhile has greatly fallen, not only because it is exhausted, but also because it is now crawling through a fully irrigated field. The mere fact of moving through an irrigated field is sufficient in itself to cost the beast its life, although with the crime of attempted flight there is no reason to look any further for violations to charge it with. Now it is dragging itself along through the mud, its four claws bogged down, sucked into the muck. But still it struggles, it throws its bones forward, and when its claws find nothing solid against which to push, the creature sticks its muzzle into the ground, its nose, its trunk, its polished head, trying to find a purchase against which to push, and flounder on. But it slips. The fully irrigated earth offers no resistance, and the animal bogs down for good.

In all the fields, the neck-ringed squads of prisoners led by the soldier-agents continue plodding on, ducking their heads and spitting in rhythmic unison. The glare of the noonday sun is blinding, and through the heat, through the shimmering squads of martially stepping prisoners, the only hint of excess or frenzy to be seen is that of the fugitive, the beast that is now burying its head completely into the mud and trying to propel its body on. Certain, therefore, that now the creature will not escape me, I move around in front of it, and I stop a few yards ahead of it, and I wait. The animal, its eyes now blinded by muck, moves heavily, squirming, using its head to drag itself forward. It writhes on, in exhausted spasms, until it bumps into something hard and solid—my feet. The fugitive raises the black ball that is its head, and it looks at me. I stand firm and rigid, and I look down on it. The fugitive buries its claws in the ground again and starts clawing, clawing, digging forward. So then to play along with it, or wear it down, or prolong its agony, or just to have some fun, or for whatever the fuck reason you may think, I turn and walk ahead a little and then I turn and stand there again, and I watch. After long and exhausting effort, it pulls itself again to the place where I am standing, and when the rodent bumps into me, it looks up again. But this time its eyes do not reach my face; they stop halfway up, apparently unable to rise any higher, and all they look at is the place where my legs come together. The squad of prisoners passes by, bowing and spitting in the shimmering glare. Then the beast, with its gaze fixed always on the same spot, starts whispering furiously. The agents, motionless, watch us from a distance. At last I react. I bend down over that head with its bulging eyes, and taking it by the neck I drag it across all the fields and through all the squads of prisoners. We return to the field it had tried to escape from. And now standing beside the great water tower I give orders that the indictment be drawn up, and I give one last glance at the fugitive reptile. Naturally, that mud-caked monster that never stops whispering as it stares fixedly at my groin is not my mother. The indictment, as befits the case, is brief and concise. A few simple *insofar as*'s and one *resolved that,* and the condemned beast is re-condemned. Among the standard clauses and conclusions, however, I instruct that there be added the charge of Criminal Deviance, for the crime of having stared fixedly at an agent-hero's fly. I sign the accusation and then I have the good fortune to be chosen to throw the criminal into the juicing tank. I do it quickly, and all the more furiously for the beast's staring at my crotch.

33

DESCRIPTION OF THE TEMPLE OF THE SUN

AND ITS GREAT RICHES

[*The Aztecs*
"Popular Reading" series]

When justice has been administered to the outlaw, I order a well-deserved inspection throughout the camp, which I declare, also with justice, *conflict-ridden.* First the agents themselves are subjected to a patriotic interrogation. Then, in numerical order by squad, a host of inmates are examined and interrogated. I am the person who examines and interrogates them—assisted, of course, by the new camp agents. I am standing to one side of the work area, and the curs are brought to me one by one. I look first of all for what interests me; that is to say, to determine whether the animal is my mother. Then immediately I begin the interrogation. With the first creature, an old male who speaks the official language (i.e., the language instituted by our glorious Represident), it looks as though the matter will be brief. The old male does not employ the proper words alone, however, following the rules of represidential language, but sometimes also lets fall two or three words outside the official vocabulary. This will cost him dear, since while new adjustments to authorized dialogues are in the process of being worked out (and have certainly not yet gone into effect), every interrogated creature must respond only with the brief authorized words or phrases, saying Yes or No as he or she is ordered. I determine, therefore, upon the sentence: Simple Annihilation in the Extractor Tank. While I stand rigidly at attention, dictating the sentence, I see that the old man, ignoring the rule that the head must be bowed to receive the sentence of law, is staring fixedly at my crotch. Outwardly controlling my rage, I order the word *Simple* scratched out and replaced by the word *Total*, and that the terrible charge of Repugnant Perversion be added. And I order the next prisoner brought to me.

34

HYPERION TO BELARMINO

[*Hyperion oder der Eremit*
Friedrich Hölderlin]

But before I examine the next prisoner, I inform the superior officers of the deviance (which we had all thought eradicated) that is rampant in the camp. I cite the examples of the fugitive and the old male just sentenced. The agents, justly terrified, listen; they know that in a camp in which this perversion is discovered, agents may find themselves seriously affected professionally, and may even be Totally Annihilated. The Represident's justice has never been stricter than in opposing this particularly horrific and grotesque crime—though for that very severity of punishment it had been thought to be eradicated from the lands of the Nation. And therefore, I exhort them, it is incumbent upon us to exterminate this plague at once, by carrying out an immediate inspection of every inmate of every camp.

35

PETER PAN APPEARS

[*Peter Pan*
J. M. Barrie]

In absolute fury, I turn to the next prisoner brought before me. I am standing, carrying out the routine interrogation. The agents scrupulously observe his eyes. I remain firm and steely as I ask my questions. The interrogation ends, and since the prisoner's eyes have remained immovably fixed on the ground during the entire examination, his original sentence is simply reaffirmed. As the next one is brought in, however, and before one word is spoken to it, the beast (a bony, putrescent reptile) fixes its eyes on my groin. Without a word, therefore, (since I am growing more enraged by the moment) I sign the order for Total Annihilation and give the prisoner a kick as I order it taken away.

The next prisoner, a young male, does not raise his eyes even to look at my face.

"The accused," I shout at the end of the interrogation, "will now hear the sentence. Raise your head."

The young prisoner opens his eyes, but he raises them no higher than my waist. Furiously I sign the order for Total Annihilation. The prisoners keep filing past. They all, incredibly, either at the beginning or the end of the interrogation, direct their eyes to the same place on my body. The situation is obviously alarming; this camp is patently perverted and corrupt beyond hope. The agents, in their zeal to aid me in stamping out this plague, write the sentence (*Total Annihilation*) on the interrogation form even before the first question.

Finally one prisoner, a common cur, sentenced to life imprisonment, does not look at the forbidden zone when he is interrogated. His old sentence is simply reaffirmed, therefore. I have completely examined him, and the beast seems normal.

The interrogations continue. The next prisoner also does not look at me. This, I think, must unquestionably be a plot. Someone, a disgusting traitor, must have given the alarm.

I give orders that any prisoner that does not look at my crotch be taken at once into the Confession Hall and be made to confess who ordered him not to look. Now, therefore, the interrogation is divided into two phases: in one, the prisoners that look at my crotch are collected to one side and sentenced to Total Annihilation and Juicing for Patriotic Irrigation; in the other phase, those that do not look are taken to one side and then led into the Hall of Confessions.

At the end of the Glorious Day (as a day's work in the field is called) my alarm has become outrage. There remain fewer than a hundred prisoners alive in all this conglomerate of fields, and they are in the process of receiving the Confession Treatment. Agents bustle about waving their arms, deploring, bewailing, moaning; some (unheard of in a Counterwhispering agent) have slit their own throats. Now to the interrogation comes the first of the survivors, those who did not look at my crotch. It seems it had detached its retinas with its own claws or had blinded itself by staring at the sun before being brought to the interrogation. Such display of temerity, such bravado, will cost these beasts dear—this is a plot, a grand conspiracy, and an act of treason.

36

THE VARIOUS KINDS OF GOVERNMENT

AND THE WAYS BY WHICH

THEY ARE ESTABLISHED

[*The Prince*
Niccolò Machiavelli]

Late that not-night, in the midst of the rumbling of the Extractors of Patriotic Juice (which are working ceaselessly throughout the entire Servo-Perimeter), I write to the High Secretary. I explain the horrendous crime I have discovered, the just and fair sentence I have handed down, and the immediacy of its execution; I disclose to him my fear that the horrendous crime has spread to, and through, every camp. *This*, I say, *is a conspiracy of the worst criminals in all of history, and as a humble soldier faithful to our glorious Represident, I propose to root out every depraved beast involved. I am prepared to disguise myself,* I say, *as one of the repugnant vermin themselves if necessary.* And I affirm, state, and declare my vow, sign and countersign it, inscribe the phrase *Long live our most glorious Represident* by my own claw upon it, and seal the missive. I send off the communiqué with the greatest urgency. And now feeling somewhat quieter, and calmed by the thunder of the Extractors, I take my rest.

REINALDO ARENAS

37

A HISTORY OF THE CONSPIRACIES

PLOTTED IN CATALONIA AGAINST

THE FRENCH ARMIES

[Huber Beaumont Brivazac]

The reply from the High Secretary arrives just as I am about to authorize numerous executions in one particularly depraved camp. The agent-mailman, who has been hurrying toward me, stops, stands at attention, and hands me the scroll with its panoply of stamps and seals. I rip off the covering, and I read: *This Great Nation takes unbounded pride in your patriotic zeal. This document is in response to your request, which we hereby grant* . . . The High Secretary himself, in person, has written this document, I realize. I look to the bottom of the scroll and I see, at the end, the Great Seal of the Office of the High Secretary. Avidly, I continue to read: . . . *In order that all may be performed properly, thoroughly, and legally, we, meeting in ministerial conclave, do hereby issue this unanimous Post-Postscript to the Postscript to the Fundamental Law, specifically Clause 112 governing Pursuit Without Respite or Quarter and Consequent Annihilation of Every Social Depravity.* The Post-Postscript reads as follows: *Regarding the concomitant corollary to that which is concluded concerning the Pursuit and Total Annihilation of any sexual deviant,* **WE HEREBY DECLARE, INCLUDE, ADD, AND AUTHORIZE** *that any person that looks, for any period of time whatsoever, however short or long, at the groin,*

crotch, thighs, or lower parts of the body, in an area com-
prised from the waist downward to the knees, of any other
citizen of our Great Nation, shall be immediately impris-
oned, and sentenced to punishment appropriate to the
crime: the criminal shall be executed as a repugnant and
repellant Beast and an Enemy of the State. Sufficient to
that sentence shall be the complaint of the gazed-upon vic-
tim. In the case that the depravedly-gazed-upon victim
should be an agent of our glorious Counterwhispering
Corps, the victim himself, should he so desire, motivated
by justifiable and reasonable patriotic indignation, may,
without fear of reprisal, immediately carry out the anni-
hilation of the depraved criminal, and then proceed to
swear out an indictment of the crime.

The Represent himself has authorized this document,
I say to myself.

And holding the great parchment in my claws, I sign the
order of execution for virtually all the prisoners in that
camp, including the agents that permitted such terrible,
and widespread, deviance. And I head for new Servo-
Perimeters, Satellite Cities, and Concentrated Rehabilitation Camps, to search out depraved beasts and destroy
them. No one will escape. No one will escape me this time.
With this document from our glorious Represent I have
in my claws the authority and the power to ferret them out
one by one, and to destroy these monsters. None will escape unscathed.

And as for my mother, the arrant whore, with the cam-
paign of patriotic purification I am planning to unleash, it
will be hard indeed for her to hide, anywhere in the Nation.
I am ready for battle now.

REINALDO ARENAS

38

MATANZAS' BREADLOAF MOUNTAIN

[An Elementary Geography of Cuba]

The Army of Moral Reconquest of the Nation is in readiness. I have chosen from the ranks of our agents those who are most physically fit and well endowed, those with long, athletic legs, firm tread, and patent sexual endowment. Their instructions are clear: Every male that looks at them in the area bounded between the knees and the waist will be subjected to Total Annihilation. Any agent looked at who, out of what will be alleged to be carelessness, does not carry out the indicated sentence will also be executed. Likewise, within that proscribed area, agents are forbidden to look *at each other*, under pain of Annihilation. And if such an act of gazing should take place (which is not expected to happen), the agent gazed at must upon the instant accuse the violator of High Crimes and Misdemeanors.

The army of slim, firm physical specimens is now standing straight and stiff before me. *To the performance of your duties,* I exhort them, *to the carrying out of justice! Inspired as you are by the heroic spirit and heroic heroism that radiates from our great hero the Supreme Represident, who has placed in our power the heroic performance of this great heroic mission—to your posts!* To the sound of a stirring and long-held *Hurrah!* the army, truly excited by its task, sets out on its mission to purify the entire Represidential Universe (i.e., the free world). I too, disguised like them as a common vermin, dressed in my baggy, faded blue multi-overalls, set out for a camp. *Even if I don't find her,*

I think, insinuating myself into a shackled squad of spitters, *the fact that with my own Claws of Power I will have annihilated so many depraved beasts will mitigate my rage at least a bit.* And at that thought, I take heart, and I continue my search for my mother.

REINALDO ARENAS

39

ATROPOS, CLOTHOS, LACHESIS,

AND ANOTHER FATE

(A RELATIVELY MINOR ONE)

NOT KNOWN UNTIL TODAY

[*The Color of Summer*
Reinaldo Arenas]

It is during the not-night, when shadows cover all the fields and work camps, and when the beasts, during the official recess, stroll in groups under the watchtowers and beside the surveillance pontoons, that the agent assigned to cruising for perverts may be most productive. Filled with energy, with his svelte, firm thighs and provocative military swagger he, too, strolls, standing out among the shaved heads whose phosphorescence glimmers through the bars and fences. If the vile and filthy creature is alone, the agent— who at no time can reveal his true identity—is allowed, in order to stimulate the criminal, to bring his claw down to his crotch and cup his groin. If the vile and filthy creature turns its head toward that zone, it may be annihilated upon the instant, and its case then sent off for bureaucratic annihilation, with the criminal's number and other vital statistics noted down on the form for official use. . . .

I walk along, just stroll along. Wearing the multi-overalls of a simple verminous beast, I walk over near a place where I see a solitary skull glimmering softly, and I stand, my legs planted far apart, close beside the polished head. A blink, a small signal, an eye that opens and that snaps shut forever.

I walk on. I leave this field and go into the next one. I leave that one, and I am in the next.

It is surprising (and truly disgusting) how many perverts our Great Nation harbors. The forms consigning criminals to Annihilation never stop coming into my agency. And the number is rising everywhere. Every crease in every piece of paper in this stack represents a depraved criminal that has had to be Annihilated. And they keep coming in, by the not-truckload. Sometimes when an agent brings in a new shipment of forms for my agency, as he unloads his cargo next to my desk he will suddenly, disgustingly, vilely, and pervertedly stare at me between the legs—and then he, too, becomes part of the unending workload. It is staggering. Sometimes whole platoons of agents, even those hand-picked to root out this crime, must be Annihilated for having stared (and this is truly alarming) not at another agent's crotch but at some simple vermin's crotch, some mere pig in the neck-chained chain gang. So as not to demoralize the Great Army, I have given orders for the gazed-at pig to be executed, as well. More and more forms full of Annihilated vermin pour in; of them, a surprising number belong to a group of agents that sent me the unbelievable request, or proposition, or supplication, or plea, or whatever the hell you call it, that they be allowed to wear special blinders to keep them from being able to look down—"so that we can avoid accidentally falling, during duty hours, into the heinous crime." That document so enraged me that besides Annihilating all the agents that wrote it, touched it, carried it, caught sight of it, etc., I drafted a counterdocument which read as follows: "As first reply, it is unheard of that one of our agents, doubly glorious—glorious first for being an agent and second for having been chosen for such a glorious assignment—should think that there exists even one second of his glorious existence when he is not on duty and at the service of his Glorious Homeland. As second reply, the fact of having proposed to wear blinders is *prima facie* proof of such ideological weakness that the proponent is revealed as a depraved and perverted criminal, for there is an implicit admission of criminal tendencies. This request, however, proposes not Annihilating the murderer but simply tying his hands behind his back. Request denied."

I sign the order for Total Annihilation of all those who collaborated in any way whatsoever in this plan, and also draft by my own claw an order that the document be done away with so that no stain may possibly remain on the Nation's character.

Even after the great execution is ended, thousands and thousands of forms continue to arrive. I pick up one at random.

Criminal number:	888-887-043-999916.
Crime:	Repugnant Criminal Depravation.
Sentence:	Total Annihilation.
Cruise Agent number:	111-454-7822, Series E.
Place in which detection occurred:	Field No. XCD HOA, Series F.
Represential Perimeter ID:	ZCX-J054.
Gazer's gaze stimulus: Degree of acuteness:	Unknown. Hard, fixed stare.
Precise location of gazer's gaze within vicinity of forbidden area:	Direct groin contact.

Bored, I return the file to the stack, and I go on with the count without looking at the details. Naturally, since these are all male criminals there is no reason for me to think I might find my mother among them. So I sit here in the huge Central Agency (surrounded by agents that look only upward, so that they are forever bumping into things and stumbling over the stacks of files), tallying and re-tallying the number of perverted, depraved criminals to whom justice has most deservedly been administered—a number that never stops growing.

40

THE LAST END

[*Singing from the Well*
Reinaldo Arenas]

As we approach the anniversary of the greatest event in the history of our Great Nation, the accession of our glorious Represident to eternal power and the consequent eternal liberation of our people, the National Children's Cooperative, in conjunction with the Communal Relations Management Agency and the represidential Office of Maximum Orientation and Supervision, has written and submitted for popular approval (for *unanimous* approval) the following draft of an Authorized Dialogue between one child and another. This dialogue will go into effect immediately upon approval, and will become the official policy of the Nation beginning on the next Represiversary; it will be followed in all children's conversations. The dialogue (with simplified wording to suit children's memories) is as follows:[1]

> *Child One:* Hip, hip, hooray!
> *Child Two:* Forever and a day!
> *Child One:* Hip, hip, hooray!

---

[1] On non-Represiversaries, children may use the dialogue during the hour of their not-nap, or for other special occasions when permission (properly signed and sealed) is obtained. On the annual Represiversary, children may dialogue freely, without special permission, and may even prolong the cheers as long as they wish.

Child Two: Forever and a day!
Both: Mister Represident, yay, yay, yay!
Child One: Ya-a-a-a-a-y![2]
Child Two: Hoora-a-a-a-a-y![3]

[2] This line shall serve as a model to be emulated in the dialogue: the child that repeats the *Hooray* or *Yay* fastest and loudest will be declared to be the winner of the dialogue.

[3] Simultaneous with *Child One*'s line, above.

41

THE FOUR GODS OF THE SKY

ACCORDING TO THE CHINESE

[*Oriental Religions*
(Author unknown)]

The examination, interrogation, and weeding out of the depraved beasts and perverts is performed now with systematic efficiency. Thanks to the trust that the High Secretary apparently places in me, I have extended the pursuit and persecution to all corners of our Nation. Now the Anti-Perversion troops, with myself at their head, traverse all the Satellite Cities and Servo-Perimeters, and we shall even come at last to the Represidential Capital itself. In this particular Perimeter where we are now working (whose major product is small placards for the Represidential Anniversary celebrations), several cases of repugnant depravity have been discovered. Its inhabitants, justifiably outraged, have volunteered to take justice into their own claws. I seize this moment of general euphoria to suggest to them the need for secret volunteer troops. That is, the members of any given level of communal organization (whether it be Satellite City, camp, or any other), wherever they may be and whatever they may be doing, may also perform the task of pervert hunting. The number of volunteers is staggering. I myself, to set the correct example, place myself at the head of one of the schools.

> *First lesson:* How the pervert-stalker walks, in order to awaken depraved appetites in the criminal.
> *Second lesson:* How the pervert-stalker is to place his claw

over his groin so that the gesture is clear to the latent
pervert without being obvious to the masses.

Third lesson: How an agent or a patriotic volunteer collab-
orator can take the depraved beast in his claw, immobilize
the criminal, and annihilate it.

When the first class of new recruits is graduated, we march
off to the next Satellite City. In this city—whose job it is,
as in so many others, to produce large placards and
posters—an irritating thing happens. At the moment of
their mass Total Annihilation, the disgusting perverts that
we have ferreted out, instead of uttering the moans of supplication and the retractations that we have planned for
them, begin to whisper. Since none of us is used to hearing
that reprehensible sound of rebellion from the enemy anymore, this action infuriates not only the agents but the
masses as well. From that whisper one might infer (and this
message has been sent directly to the High Secretary) that
every Depraved Criminal is something even worse—a po-
litical enemy, an enemy of our glorious Represident, and,
therefore, an enemy of the Entire Glorious Nation. The persecution now has a double objective: both moral and polit-
ical. More training troops are added. Night and day we
advance, firm and watchful, our legs spread wide, our claws
squeezing our sexual bulges (which some agents have made
even more prominent with socks or a stone of the proper
shape and weight). The hymns of General Purification are
sung by the masses and played on loudspeakers across the
land. We never rest.

Every day I file my report on the political-pervert criminals to whom justice has deservedly been administered. But
the most alarming thing about this situation, I write at the
end of one day's report, is that the number of depraved
whispering criminals does not decrease with our persecution, it appears to grow. At the very end of my report, under
the seal on top of my signature, I allow myself to make a
non-general comment: *My mother,* I report to the High Secretary, *has not yet been found.*

42

THUS SPEAK THE GODS OF THE GANGES:

THE GREAT REPAY NO FAVORS

OF THE HUMBLE

[Twenty Stories from India
(Various)]

I am in this remote Satellite City, hundreds of leagues from the Represidential Capital, and I suddenly receive a telegram from the High Secretary, with the military stamp of the High Secretary's office officially affixed. *The Represident is proud of your work,* it reads. *On His behalf, receive the grateful homage of Our Nation. Long live our heroes.* And below, in the same claw-writing, an unofficial note: *Do not yield in the search for your parent.*

This roll of parchment is very, very significant to me. I read it again. I roll it and unroll it. With my strong legs spread wide, I stroll through this remote Satellite City. I look up at the not-night, and I once again unroll the roll. What do I care what the Represident thinks? What do I care about the opinion of one pig more, his hatred or his congratulations? What moves me is the note at the end from the High Secretary: *Do not yield in the search for your parent.* If the High Secretary in person (and I stroll along in a state of great arousal, squeezing my member with my claw, watchful for the slightest glance that might light upon my groin) . . . If the High Secretary in person, I think, advises me not to yield in my search for my mother, it is because he knows that I will find her yet. . . . Once again I hold up the parchment to look at it, once again I read it. I walk quickly, and in the shadows of the not-night I whisper softly, sibilantly, slyly. Tomorrow I will have all the vermin in this entire Satellite City executed for whispering. Tomorrow, nothing. This very minute. Now. And to avoid any possibility of anti-genocidal mitigation, I once again pollute the not-night with my long-drawn-out whisper.

43

IN WHICH IS DESCRIBED THE LOCATION, SIZE, AND SHAPE OF THE ISLAND

[A Description of The Island of Cuba
Nicolás Joseph Ribera]

DECREE

In accord with the new Plan for the Socio-Economic Development of the Nation, and taking into account the high level of politico-cultural development already achieved by the masses, their firm and upright ideology, their deep-seated sense of humanity, the Nation's plans for the development of relations tending both toward universal fraternity and toward strengthening the militant ideology of every citizen, and above all as a basic tribute to this year's anniversary of the Represident's infinite triumph and of his humane initiatives, and in consonance with his great analytical, synthetical, predictive, and supervisory abilities,

IT IS HEREBY DECREED,

by order of the Represident himself and at his behest (upon stamping and sealing the appropriate orders to that effect), that the *FIRST UNIVERSAL AUTHORIZED DIALOGUE*, to be spoken (at the appropriate time, place, and date) by a man and a woman, shall be immediately put into force. The authorities entertain the highest confidence that the conscience of the citizenry will shun any sort of deviation, amendment, or omission whatsoever from its specific terms, under penalty of People's Justice. The dialogue, exhaustively planned, revised, and fitted to the needs of our Nation and to our exalted spirit of struggle and creation, is to be employed on the occasion of the upcoming Represiversary by all citizens named or referred to in this decree (i.e., all citizens of the free world), and reads as follows:

Man:	Long live our glorious Represident!
Woman:	Hurray, hurray, hurray, hurray.
Man:	With dedication, more production.
Woman:	Production, production, production.
Man:	More efficiency, increased decency.
Woman:	Decency, decency.
Man:	Grr, grr, grr, annihilate the enemy.
Woman:	Grr, grr, grrrr.
Man:	Tolerate neither weakness, nor rest, nor groin-ward gaze so sinister.
Woman:	Grr, grr, grrr.
Man:	Our claws united against the whisperer.
Woman:	Grr, grr, grrr.
Man:	Our claws linked in chains against the backslider.
Woman:	Grr, grr, grrr.
Man:	Our claws like vises for the sick and malingerers.
Woman:	Grr, grr, grrr.
Man:	Our claws like garrotes for represidential traitors.
Woman:	Grr, grr, grrr.
Man:	Grr, grr, grrr.
Together:	Grr, grr, grrr.

FIRST POSTSCRIPT:
On the day of the Great Assembly, the *grr*'s shall be repeated louder and louder until they echo in every corner of the Nation, and make every Enemy of the People tremble.

SECOND POSTSCRIPT:
The other portions of the dialogue shall be repeated exactly as set forth above. Only in case of maximum emotion may the number of *grr*'s be increased. [A] Experiments of author-

ized copulation performed with certain couples have clearly shown greater intensity, and therefore greater effectiveness, when union can be achieved at the same time as the *grr*'s are being pronounced and when the time of the union can be reduced to five minutes or less. [B] Nonetheless, let it be clear that in order to perform the coupling at the same time as the couple is softly uttering the *grr*'s, there is required, over and above the standard official permission, the Represident's own symbolic permission, which may be requested at any regional or zonal office. [C] Insofar as the lengthening or truncation of the model dialogue is concerned, or any other change to, or mutilation of, it, any person who commits this offense shall be charged, tried, found guilty of, and sentenced for a crime against the State (Counter-patriotism), an offense which shall henceforth be included in the clause for "Capital Offenses, No Mitigating Circumstances Considered."

44

THE PART WHICH DIVINE PROVIDENCE
PLAYED IN MY PROFESSION AS AUTHOR

[*The Mystics*
(Various)]

While visiting these Servo-Perimeters with their Satellite Cities specializing in the manufacture of medium-sized placards and posters, I discover a new mode of criminal depravity. The weight of the placard sometimes makes the rodent in charge of waving it around crouch down in order to lift it up. Just as this happened in one instance, I saw the pervert behind the placard waver look not at the placard, which was what the pervert should have been looking at, but at the placard waver's backside. Wearing my simple-citizen's multi-overalls, I followed along, like any simple citizen, waving my medium-sized placard, and secretly keeping my eye on the eyes of the citizens that were following the squatting-backside placard waver. They were not only watching that backside, but the longer they watched it the more negligently they performed their duties. And their excitation raised a great bulge in the state overalls. I became so enraged that I could not control myself another second. I raised the alarm. The first criminal was thrown in chains, and at once the beast was given the required clubbing and then the *coup de grace.* What was so incredible about all this was that even as he was receiving his beating, he maintained his erection (and I believe it even grew).

So since I have discovered this new type of perversion, I

have given orders to address it, requiring that any person, including women as well as men, who shall look upon the backside of another person, whether man or woman, shall immediately be Annihilated. In order to apprehend this sort of criminal we have had to redouble our surveillance, because although before the discovery of this new perversion, the person-looked-at-with-perverted-intent could be both police officer and witness, now, since the person is being looked at from behind, that method has become patently impossible. Of course the most perspicacious agents now always walk half sideways, with one eye looking backward, and this method has yielded good results.

A problem remains, however. The criminal epidemic has affected not just this Servo-Perimeter, but apparently is much more widespread, and may even have become general. I have reported the discovery of this new crime to the High Secretary, vowing that on the day of the celebration of the Represidential Anniversary, the Nation will have been rid once and for all of all criminal depravity. And without more ado I march to the head of the secret troops, who by my order have emphasized not only their groins but also their backsides, using rags, sawdust, polished marble, clay, wire, or whatever the hell else they feel like, goddammit.

45

THE TERRIFYING STORM THAT OCCURRED IN GUATEMALA, IN WHICH DOÑA BEATRIZ DE LA CUEVA LOST HER LIFE

[*Historia general de las Indias*
Francisco López de Gómara]

In its constant concern for the dignity and purity of the Represident's Great Nation, the Senate Patriotic Committee for Oversight of the Nation's Morality, having learned of this new criminal deviance that has become so egregiously manifest to our Patriotic Vanguard, and wishing to eliminate this threat before the day of this year's Represiversary (so that our Great Nation, free of all perversion and depravity, can once again fly its flag proudly), has requested that the High Secretary issue the following resolution:

RESOLVED that:
Any criminal who shall look, whether carelessly, fixedly, directly, out of the corner of his or her eye, or through lowered lids, whether for a long period of time or fleetingly or for the merest microsecond, at the buttocks of one of his or her fellow citizens, shall be, without further processing, subjected to the strictest rigor of the law, which is the sentence and execution of Annihilation and Erasure forever from the rolls of Our Great Family. Long live our glorious Represident, all hail to the next shining Anniversary.

46

JALISCO

[*Historia general de las Indias*
Francisco López de Gómara]

There is not much time. Everywhere, in every part of the Nation, all one hears, even among the rocks and dust clouds, is the sound of placards being nailed to long sticks of wood, posters being nailed to walls, flags being nailed up everywhere, and panels and mini-panels being nailed together to form reviewing stands. As the Represidential Anniversary approaches, all one hears is the sound of hammering, sawing, wood being planed, cans and oil drums being banged on as the new anthems are rehearsed, cloths, rags, and leather goods being shaken out, great flags bellying and snapping in the wind, the goose-stepping of citizens rehearsing and re-rehearsing their marches, and the clubbing, ever faster, of the heads of perverts by the pervert hunters. There is not much time left. At the head of the great Anti-Perversion Brigade, I am the scourge of the Servo-Perimeters, the Satellite Cities, and the work camps. In each triumphant battle I avidly search for the backside of my mother, the stony face of my mother, the claw-fingered hands of my mother, and the cow's eyes that my mother used to look at me with (which are now almost my own claw-fingered hands and my own watery bovine eyes). Never finding her, I go on signing sentences of execution. Dealing out patriotic kicks right and left, I once again rage through every part of the Nation. The hammering is now deafening. Everywhere the vermin have been assigned permanent shifts, and anyone caught sleeping is Annihilated.

All our forces are joined and multiplied in the service of the preparations for this year's Represiversary, which is to be the grandest ever.

Through waves of that shrieking, banging euphoria (after having purified the Great Nation), I triumphantly enter the Represidential Capital. (I have still found not the slightest trace of my mother.) By express order of the High Secretary, whose communiqué calls me a Represidential Hero, I am invited to the Office of the High Secretary, where I am to receive a hero's honors. Growling softly, I stalk through the barred gates of the great estate, looking closely at every guard (all of whom quickly and servilely bow)—but none of them is her, the bitch is nowhere to be found—and I enter the great Hall of Receptions, where the Great Secretary in person, seeing me from afar, stands to greet me.

47

OF HOW, BECAUSE OF THE GREAT LUST

WHICH THEY HAVE,

WOMEN MAKE LOVE RIGHT AND LEFT

[El Corbacho ("The Goad")
The Archpriest of Talavera]

COMMUNIQUE NO. 1

Upon the occasion of the act of homage to the Represident soon to be held, and in order to provide orientations to all inhabitants of Our Great Nation as to the manner in which our glorious Represident is to be rendered the honors which are due him, the following guidelines are issued. These guidelines shall be strictly observed by every member of the Nation, who shall on the day in question be prostrated, as all the free universe must be, before the Represidential Reviewing Stand.

A) One day before the Glorious Day, the entire community of the free universe shall remain unanimously on its feet and in silence, in rehearsal for the minute of silence which will be accorded the Represident when he appears upon the dais.

B) When the period of silence is ended, all members of the free universe shall make their way, dressed in their multioveralls, to their respective monolithic formations, and from there they shall monolithically depart for the Great National Patriotic Square. When the individual monolithic formations begin their march, they shall give a Great Patriotic Cheer.

C) On the way to the Great National Patriotic Square, each footstep of each monolithic formation shall be taken with the member's eyes fixed on the sky, and in this posture, without any deviation or detour, they shall cry out the Great Patriotic Cheer. Between one monolithic formation and another there shall be permitted only the space necessary for each formation representative to execute his or her respective maneuvers.

D) Every member of every formation (that is, every inhabitant of the free universe) shall carry a flag, pennant, placard, banner, streamer, or poster, and shall carry this flag, pennant, placard, etc. in one hand or in two, with the teeth or with the head, according to the Procession Pre-Plan. Under no circumstances shall the flags, pennants, placards, etc. be lowered even for an instant, and any infraction of this rule shall be subject to the severest penalty. Any member of the procession who because of the type of flag, pennant, placard, banner, etc. carried must carry it in the teeth must not for that reason cease crying out *Hurrah!* at the appropriate moments, or those moments indicated by the formation leader, and must at all times strive to increase the height and firmness of the flag, pennant, placard, etc. which he or she carries, as well as to keep his or her gaze fixed firmly upon the empyrean.

E) The march to the Great National Patriotic Square shall be performed with a constant rhythm and motion, with no movement except those sanctioned by these regulations. Any member of the procession who scratches, looks about, talks, etc. shall be reported for subsequent execution, once the Assembly and Honors have been concluded.

F) The formations, upon arriving at the Square, shall take their places in the designated locations, following the large Guide Placard that precedes them. They shall stand motionless until the remaining formations occupy their respective locations. Each member of each formation shall take precautions to ensure the well-being of his or her flag, pennant, banner, etc.; the slightest damage or dent to the aforementioned object shall be reason to be reported for execution.

G) Once the entire free universal world is standing in its designated place, every member of every formation shall wait, at absolute attention, for the entrance of the President, which may or may not be immediate. Whether delay occurs or not, this point must be most strictly observed.

H) In accordance with the instructions given by the Director of the Ceremony, the hurrahs, anthems, vivas, or *grr*'s shall be repeated each time the signal is given, throughout the President's speech, which shall last approximately thirty hours. Then, at a subsequent signal from the President himself, adoration of him shall be expressed in the usual forms. Generally speaking, this passion may be expressed freely, each member of the Assembly choosing his or her own mode: writhing, twisting about, bowing, jumping up and down, masturbating, cutting one's own throat, striking or hitting oneself, putting out one's eye (or eyes), as a proof of worshipful sacrifice. But at no time shall the worshiper abandon his or her assigned position. The euphoria and delirium of the adoration shall last as long as the President's ecstasy at being worshiped. Once his ecstasy has concluded, the universal represidential anthem shall be played, and shall be observed at attention. Then each member of the Assembly shall, within his or her own respective block, hand in his or her respective flag, banner, placard, etc., and shall return immediately to his or her respective patriotic labors.

48

THE SEXUAL USE OF THE ANAL ORIFICE

[The Erotic Bible
Gustave Mirabeau]

I enter Represidential Headquarters. At the far end of a great hall the High Secretary is sitting at his desk. When he sees me, he rises to his feet. He puts out his claw. The claw is red because of the piece of cloth that is wrapped around it. All his underlings' claws are that color red too, because all their claws are likewise wrapped in that same kind of red cloth. When the High Secretary stands, all the agents, which means all the personnel in the entire Headquarters, also rise to their feet. I remain standing as well, waiting for the High Secretary. I think, seeing the important-looking red scribble he writes, that after the Represident, he's number one. Everyone knows that if the Represident should die, disappear, perish, pop, or how the hell should I know what might happen to him (since it is unthinkable anyway), this man would be number one. It's logical, then, that he has to watch out for the Represident, I think. Although it's even more logical, I think, that the Represident (who is currently Number One) ought to watch out for this one and only vice–number one, who would be number one if something happened to number one.

Now he hands me the order. At a gesture of his red-upholstered claw for me to step up to his great desk, I step forward. I am standing before his great desk. The minor beasts all bow. The High Secretary, across the desk covered with gewgaws, stretches his paws out even farther, and he embraces me. His eyes, which look directly at me without the slightest sign of wavering, are large, bright, and a little red, perhaps because of so much red all around. While still embraced by him, and without waiting another moment, I say what I have to say: *I still haven't found her. I have looked for her everywhere, and I still haven't found her.* The High Secretary keeps looking at me. Then, throwing one of his claws over my shoulder, he walks with me all along the side of the great desk. Everyone stands rigid, watching us stroll.

"The Nation," he says to me, "is very, very grateful to you for your heroic service. The Represent in person has ordered me to convey to you that thanks."

Now he stops. We stop. One of his claws rises. Instantly there is a sound of trumpets or cornets or conch shells or empty pipes or how the hell should I know what was making the fucking noise, and silence falls.

The High Secretary says, "My friend, it is my honor to declare you, by order of our glorious Represent, Great Hero of the Nation. Please receive your grateful country's thanks."

That bleating noise again. A small squad of agents perfectly dressed in red—young men, boys almost—approach us, shaking their asses and showing off their legs and groins. All the personnel in the office stand as though in a trance watching the little greeting committee walk toward us with a huge tray or long board in their claws. I think, seeing everyone looking at the bulging groins of these young men, that that act alone would be enough, if it weren't for the people involved, to condemn them all, including the High Secretary himself, to Total Annihilation. And I have to restrain myself from shouting: *Seize those perverted criminals!* The group of young men is now standing before us. Now, from the center of the group there steps out one soldier, clearly well endowed, with the panel or board or tray or whatever the hell it is in his claws. Wriggling in his tight-fitting uniform, he steps up to me. No one is looking at the piece of tin he is carrying on the tray; everyone is looking at the young body inside that uniform, so firm and full of life that it seems to be trying to wriggle out of it. The High Secretary, far from examining the piece of tin, examines the body of the patriotic young soldier. His gaze rises to his face. And then the two gazes, that of the patriotic soldier and that of the High Secretary, meet in a look of complicity. The patriotic soldier's eyes, moist and yielding, are like those of an animal that knows itself desired; the eyes of the High Secretary are smiling, and he bats his eyelashes. At last the soldier smiles back, his heavy dewlaps stretch. The moment seems endless to me. The soldier stands firm and straight (while everyone looks at him), holding the enormous board. The Secretary puts out both claws to pick up the piece of tin. As he picks it up, the four claws (Secretary claws and soldier claws) touch. And now the High Secretary, achieving that light, but obvious, touch of the claw, turns and looks at me.

"You have performed great deeds," he says. And I can see the mockery in his eyes, the mockery of me.

Now the claw wrapped in red cloth picks up the gleaming piece of tin and carries it solemnly to my chest. The silence is absolute. The High Secretary's claws, maneuvering with some difficulty (no doubt because of the red cloth), pin the sparkling piece of tin to my chest. Finally the operation is completed, and he says:

"By express order of the Represident, I have awarded you the Medal of National Represidential Heroism."

When his speech is ended, the High Secretary puts both claws on my shoulders again and symbolically embraces me. *I haven't been able to find her*, I say again, softly yet firmly. The embrace ends, but with both claws still on my shoulders he looks with satisfaction at the enormous medal he has just pinned to my uniform. And he says to me aloud:

"I have the infinite honor to inform you that by express order of the Represident you are invited to be guest of honor upon the Great Represidential Reviewing Stand, where you will once again be symbolically awarded this medal by the

Represident himself, and simultaneously declared, to all the world, a Hero of the Universe."

The cheering is unanimous. The soldier remains firmly planted before us, looking at the High Secretary and holding the tray. At a gesture from the High Secretary the cheering ends, and the High Secretary takes me by the shoulder and ushers me from the hall. We walk down the hallway lined with trophies, busts, statues, and monuments to the Represident and we come out onto a sort of balcony, or railing, or fire escape, or stage above the city. Down below, vermin scurry, stagger, carry, lift, squat, stop, stoop, stand, nail and tear down, put on and take off, throw up reviewing stands and pull them down again—in a word, make preparations for the great festivities, for the great day which is now so rapidly approaching. The anthems echo throughout the city. And from up where we are standing it looks as though that scurrying mob of vermin down there is moving in time to the constantly louder, constantly more excited noise of the anthems, in time to all that screeching. The High Secretary leans one claw against a column and in a sort of ecstasy contemplates that grand panorama. Thousands of ratlike creatures are carrying a gigantic, cumbersome object through the city, a huge sculpture of the Represident surrounded by the sun, the moon, and a monumental star. Sometimes the awkward weight of the thing makes it swing wildly, bump against the ground or a wall, and lose its balance, squashing a hundred or a thousand of the scurrying drones. These disembowelings seem to bring the High Secretary out of his trance, for now, seeing yet another bloody accident involving the bearers of the enormous statue, he makes a face almost of mockery, and calls me over to his side.

"We could have done other things," he says to me. "We could have left the trees, for example, let the countryside flower, filled everybody's belly. But if people had full bellies, and leisure and shade and places to go on their vacations, and free time to indulge in philosophical discussions or even to get bored in, and to weigh things and compare things, and then finally to start worrying and feeling Angst and ennui and Weltschmerz and other foreign emotions—if they had all that, do you think they'd worship us the way they do? Do you believe that a person who can choose, a person who is free, can bear to see other people who cannot choose, who are not free? What we had to do—and this the Represident knows well—was undermine everything, destroy everything that represented balance, that offered a point of comparison, that symbolized stability, that stood in our memories—demolish everything that might have represented the center, coherence, order, a system of values, and then begin anew, creating a new kind of balance, founded precisely on *im*balance, on the loss of the true center. When a man, or that thing you see down there below, knows that in the time between one spit and another all he can count on is the possibility of accumulating a little bit of saliva so he can spit again, there's nothing to fear from him. Ah, but if you give him a rest, a little vacation, if you let him fulfill himself, if you don't put a stop to his philosophical discussions in time, if you allow him to think, to criticize, then sooner or later he'll discover that you, who allow him to exist, are his worst enemy, and he will rise up in rebellion against you who gave him the gift of freedom, and he will acquire such strength that you will not be able to stop him—how can you, if precisely by doing so you would be going against your own principles? And at last he will annihilate you. There will be nothing left of your high principles; he will trample them down like an ox or a sow. And after a few noisy kicks right and left and all over the place, he will return to being that thing you see down there, a clumsy beast, a docile, stinking verminous beast of burden that you can load and unload at will. . . .

"That being the case, and you know that that *is* the case," he goes on, looking at me fixedly once more, "what is one to do but try not to get caught up in the confusion, try to stay above it, to be, in fact, the master of it . . . What is one to do but pick up the lash, quick, before somebody beats you to it and whips you back into the herd?"

We continue our walk. I try to tell him that I understand perfectly, but that I am not in the least interested, that I have a different problem. But the High Secretary, taking me by the arm, goes on talking as we stroll along the immense balcony.

"You know that many people have already forgotten the spoken language. In the last census, it was discovered that most people use no more than thirty or forty words their whole life long. The official dialogues solve that problem. Whether people know the language or not doesn't matter. In fact, in terms of the faithful repetition of the official dialogues, it's much better that they be absolutely ignorant of the language—there'll never be any mistakes that way, or additions, or interpolations. . . . And anyone that does try to change the dialogues around or take words out of context will have to suffer the consequences from those who only know the official words—which of course is virtually everyone. . . . And to tell the truth," he says, now stopping in the center of an open gallery, "what have we done here but accomplish a great deal of good? Why, what does man pursue if not peace and tranquillity. What else have all the sages and wise men of all the ages—whom you will no longer know anything about, I imagine, or maybe you do, I don't know—what else have they sought (and quite fruitlessly, I might add) but an end to that blind uncertainty that for every intelligent man life was. We have discovered and brought to the world what no philosopher, sage, or humanist has ever been able to find. We have discovered harmony, universal equilibrium. Yes, universal—for soon the universe will be but one great, unanimous murmur that rises and falls, or falls utterly silent, in a rhythm which is perfectly regulated, at a location which is predetermined. It will soon be one unanimous breath that rises or ceases in response to one control, one unassailable plan. And no one will have any reason for regret, no one will have anything to complain about, there will be nothing to reject or to object to, because no one will know anything but that plan, repeated, and repeated, and repeated. . . . Philosophy, hope, anguish, freedom? Don't all those notions sound ridiculous to you? Do you really care about them, or take that rhetoric seriously? Because if you, who are one of the elite of our Nation, don't take them seriously, do you think, then, that *they* care, that anthill of creeping drones down there struggling with that scaffolding, who'll then wrestle another into place, and another, and another? . . . Are you familiar with the dialogue between the man and woman? What do you think of it?"

I can only nod. I want to say something about my mother, which is what I'm really interested in, but he keeps talking.

"Well, a dialogue is being drafted," he says to me in a confidential tone, "which is intended just for men. What do you think of *that*? Do you think once that dialogue becomes official there will be any other itch, shall we call it, that will still be unsatisfied? In fact, the news was so incredible for those masses down there that when they heard it they tried to murder the agent that told them, because they all thought he was a traitor. Imagine, a dialogue between men . . . What do you think of that?"

"That's fine," I nod.

"But there's another thing," the High Secretary goes on, "something much more important, something that will bring to its final culmination the universal equilibrium that all men everywhere have desired. Listen—and this is a confession—there is a plan in the works, in fact it's in the final stages of approval, that would allow one member of the communal group to legally eat another member if it can be demonstrated that the member to be eaten is an Enemy of the People and if his or her body is requisitioned to be salted and eaten. What do you think of that? Wouldn't that be absolute equilibrium? Do you think that a state can have anything to fear from any of its citizens when the citizens' greatest concern will be watching out that other citizens don't eat them? . . . Ha ha ha. Look how they obey, look how rhythmically they bow down, squat down, push, lift, carry. They are absolutely euphoric! Believe it or not, they are happy. Yes, happy. In the past the error of all leaders was to think that in order to remain in power they had to make concessions, to give and give and give. . . . But success lies in just the opposite. The secret is to take away—take away more and more and more, until the very freedom to continue to breathe the stinking polluted air, to live a life of submission, is so uncertain that in order to earn that freedom, however precarious it may be, every person will find joy in betraying every other person, eating every other person, and for that they will even patiently wait their turn. . . . Look at them, just look at them. They are a herd, a pack of madmen, of poor beasts, of starving slaves, blind and stinking and wretched, but it is a fiesta too, it looks like a veritable party. . . ."

And I look down at that immense herd scurrying about unceasingly down there below. There is such uniformity in their rhythm, in their movements, I think, that it truly does look like some sort of dance. . . .

"And it *is*," the High Secretary says to me, once again laying his huge red claw on my shoulder. "It is the largest and most macabre, the most uniform and perfect, most drawn-out, dizzying, and well-performed dance that has ever been danced in the universe. . . ."

I look again at that stiff face now gazing down in ecstasy upon the herd. I am certain I didn't speak, yet he answered me. . . .

"High Secretary," I then say, for the first time genuinely respectful, "the Represident's wisdom is infinite. . . . That is why I thought that I might, through your good offices, request authorization to be given a permit to have an audience with the Represident to ask him a question."

Turning his back to the square across which the vermin were madly scurrying, the High Secretary speaks:

"The Represident's wisdom is great," he says. And then he adds, "The Represident's, and my own."

And as he says these last words his voice becomes thunderous, and he stands even more stiffly and erectly.

"What is it that you really want?" he says then.

"High Secretary," I say, "from you I cannot hide, and have not hidden, the reasons that drove me to become a Hero of the State. You know what motives, what desires— though still unsatisfied—have inspired me. You know," and now I am virtually pleading with him, "that all I truly want is to find my mother and destroy her. Everything I have done has been with that end in mind. And now that I have traveled the entire Universe, eliminating beasts and vermin, and still not found her, how can I go on living, how, *why* should I go on, how can I bear to wear this medal, accept this honor, listen to these praises, if they represent for me worse than mockery—defeat? How can I go on, if I know that the beast that I pursue is there, down there somewhere, plotting against me, laughing at me, getting farther and farther under my skin, deeper and deeper inside me, until she becomes me myself, until she at last completely disfigures me and I become her. And I can do nothing but pursue and kill those that are not her, until at last, in order to kill her, I will have to kill myself, while she remains forever alive, laughing, looking out through her mask at this thing that I am. High Secretary," I plead, "tell me where she is, where my mother is. And if you do not know, grant me the High Authorization to ask the Represident. He surely knows, he has to. . . ."

The High Secretary, standing before me, looks at me as though he is studying me. Then, still staring at me, he says:

"If there is anyone that has tried to aid you in this undertaking, it has been I. Do not forget that. I understand you perfectly. All this time I have watched you, I have observed you, I have personally studied you, and I understand you. I know that your intentions are real, for they are based on hate. Tomorrow, you may have your wish. . . ." The

High Secretary turns once more to look down on the millions of vermin scurrying about beneath his feet. "You are one of our guests of honor, and you will occupy, on the Represident's orders, a place on the Fourth Heroic Reviewing Stand. Your mother is supposed to be there too. And you will see her. . . . What a wonderful day, what a grand, grand day," says the High Secretary, turning his back to me and speaking as though into the Infinite. And I watch as he stretches out his claws, as though possessed, and walks away for a few steps. Then, returning and placing both claws on my shoulders, he says:

"Now, off with you. Get ready for the ceremony."

And without another word he turns, walks the full length of the long hallway, or corridor, or great arcade, or whatever the hell you call it, and disappears into the immense Hall of Receptions.

49

GENETIC APPLICATIONS TO THE YIELD

OF VARIOUS ZOOGENETIC SPECIES

[Applied Husbandry
(Various)]

COMMUNIQUE NO. 94

IN RE: Sub-Sub-Paragraphs (A) and (B) of Sub-Paragraph (B) of Paragraph (H) of the Regulations Governing the Represidential Anniversary Assembly. The following sub-clauses and preconditions to be included. These rules and regulations shall be strictly observed during the celebration of the Represidential Anniversary Assembly.

Paragraph (H), Sub-Paragraph (B), Sub-Sub-Paragraph (A), as amended
[**Governing the speech:**] When the glorious figure of the Represident appears, all citizens of the entire free universe shall, unanimously, raise above themselves, and wave, whatever signs or insignia they shall possess, whether flags, pennants, banners, placards, posters, etc., and shall begin to wave those insignia about at the same time as, opening their mouths, they shall shout *Hurrah, hurrah, hurrah!* When the three hurrahs have ended, they shall lower their heads until the tips of their noses shall touch the ground. Then, at the sound of the patriotic whistle, they shall execute a rapid leap to their feet and, standing stiffly at attention, in their original positions, they shall shout *Hurrah* three more times. This series of actions shall be performed without pause, exactly as described, and shall be

continued repeatedly until the Represident shall with his great libertarian hand signal a cessation of this activity. Then the assembly shall begin to applaud with both claws (all the patriotic insignia, etc., being held in the teeth) at an average of three claw claps per second; the sound of these claw claps shall gradually increase in volume until the Represident, with his great libertarian hand, shall signal a cessation of this activity. The subsequent silence shall then be absolute, until the commencement of the chanting of the great Patriotic Slogan, which for this year's anniversary shall be: *Represident for everybody, Represident for every need, Represident forever!* When the chanting of the slogan has ended, the Moment of Patriotic Delirium shall begin. Every member of the Nation shall have the right to demonstrate his or her worship of the Represident as frenziedly as possible: the members shall jump up and down on one foot or on two, stand on their heads or get down on all fours, shout *Viva-viva-viva* wildly and uninterruptedly, or make any bodily offering desired, such as, for example, an arm, an eye, a foot, a finger, or even the heart. It is required that all offerings made by members of the Patriotic Assembly shall be directed toward the Represident (that is, thrown before the Main Represidential Reviewing Stand), but under no circumstances, whatever the offering may be, whatever the shouting and frenzy, shall any member step outside the strict location of his or her formation. When the offerings and worship are concluded (that is, when the Represident has signaled that the offerings and worship shall be ended), the National Anthem shall be played. And immediately the entire free universe shall shout: *Glory to the Represident who has brought glory to our glorious land.* And then the National Heroes, honored to be so honored, shall be called up, and they shall come forward, in strict order as they are called, from their respective Secondary, Tertiary, Fourth- and subsequent-Degree Reviewing Stands, and make their way toward the Main Represidential Reviewing Stand where the Represident shall be awaiting them to perform the symbolic act of their Heroic Investiture. Meanwhile, the mass shall, unanimously, be shouting *Hurrah-hurrah-hurrah,* and shall be applauding with their two claws, and shall be waving their respective insignia (flags, banners, placards, posters, etc.) with their teeth. When the Grand National Ceremony of Bestowal of Decorations has concluded, the forty anthems chosen in honor of the Represidential Anniversary shall be sung and played, and then once again there shall be celebrated a minute of silence in honor of the heroes fallen in the Great Patriotic National Clean-Up, this minute to be observed at strict attention. Then there shall be broadcast from every loudspeaker in the free universe a patriotic voice, which shall make the following announcement: *The highest and most unsurpassable moment which the worldwide free universe can arrive at has arrived. The entire worldwide world awaits in great anticipation the words of our worldwide hero. The Great Represident shall now speak.*

And the Represident's speech shall begin.

50

ON MY FILMS

[Charles Chaplin]

Not-night. Tomorrow will be the Big Day. Tomorrow, the High Secretary tells me, I will be able to see her. I will be able to take her in my claws and rip her throat out. Slash her jugular. Decapitate her. I am in my glass house, where I have come to lie down and rest while the masses are standing in silence rehearsing the patriotic Minute of Silence, and I think that she is out there somewhere in that rigid multitude, and I can hardly control myself. In fact, if it were not for the strict orders not to interrupt the national rehearsal for the Minute of Silence (which is to last the entire not-night) under any circumstances, I would set out this very instant to try to find her. But I wait. I am lying here on my back with my eyes open. She is out there, she is nearby, she is coming. She stands before me. She spreads her huge horrible legs and she pees. The stream of urine floods over me, and I run, gasping from the smell of piss. I run, but the old she-mule, standing there in front of me, spreads her huge horrible legs again, and I see before my eyes the gigantic clutch of hair, always hovering before me like some monstrous spider, gnawing, gobbling, writhing. I run, run. And the spider, rising on its uprights, whistles, wheezes, bleats, and, seizing me in its hot legs, pours down on me the filthy bloody flux of its menstruation. I open my eyes, I scream, and beating my face with my claws I jump out of bed. There, outside the window, is the sky. The sky with all its gewgaws and accoutrements—stars, twinkly planets, comets, and its biggest gewgaw of all, the moon.

The horrible moon, with its round, swollen face, the matronly, jeering face of a cheap aging whore, a dirty, frigid whore that looks dazed and half stupid from being kicked around so much. I look at her, she looks at me, the horrible disk of her face stoops down to my body, and she slaps me. Then, rising again, she gives that falsetto shriek, and she just sits there, up there in the sky, still looking at me, wheezing, gasping, and breathless. The hairs on my neck and head stand on end, my arms rise, my claws rise, my talons rise and rip out my hair, which in less than a second grows back and rises on end again. Up there in the sky, the immense red-colored gewgaw is now a huge hairy suppurating mound of flesh. And it squirts at me the horrible muck of a redder and redder, more and more monstrous menstruation. The nauseating liquid flows over my face. The stinking blood and pus cover me. I claw at my face, I leap up, I run, but the liquid goes on flooding me. The hairy monster keeps squirting me. *Mother, mother,* I cry. And she swallows me, she keeps drowning me, transfixing me. Now she has totally covered me, negated me, buried me, turned me into something soft and trembling and unformed, turned me into another suppurating hairy mound crying *Mother, mother.* And so I drip heavy drops of blood; I am bleeding, drooling, calling out, crying out, drowning in a sticky viscous hairy pool. And her, up there in the sky, round and whorish—she squirts another stream of menstrual blood, suddenly lighting the darkness of my horror, making me see, now, as she does. I . . . She . . . Screaming, I leap up again, grab up my Claw of Power, and run outside. I have to kill her, I have to kill her *now.* And howling, leaping, screaming, I am outside.

At that very moment there bursts forth the sound of the anthems announcing the dawn of the Great Day, and the twelve-hour rehearsal for the Minute of Silence is ended. Men and women are running to find their formations. I control myself, I go back into my house of glass, I put away the Claw of Power that I absolutely cannot take with me to the Assembly, and I go outside again, even more angrily now, and start toward the Grand National Patriotic Square. Looking for her, looking for that whore, looking for my last chance to find her and annihilate her, looking for her, the miserable bitch. Trembling in fury and rage and terror, now almost running, I come to the Square and take my place on the Fourth-Degree Represidential Reviewing Stand, reserved for the Heroes of the Nation.

51

GROWING UNEASINESS.

THE GRANDPARENTS AND THE

BOAT RIDE AT DUSK

[The Magic Mountain
Thomas Mann]

COMMUNIQUE NO. 94
(CONT'D.)

Paragraph (H), Sub-Paragraph (B), Sub-Sub-Paragraph (B), as amended
[**Governing the post-speech period:**] After the Represident's Official Speech, no one shall speak for thirty days about anything but the brilliant speech (and then, only during Authorized Conversation Periods). The words that may be used are the following: *glorious, wonderful, great, unique, optimistic, and magnanimous.* The word *very* may be combined with any of the above. At the conclusion of these thirty days of praise, the Official Dialogues shall begin to be observed, which within that time shall have been memorized by every member of the Nation. Employing any dialogue other than the Official Dialogue shall be considered conspiratorial activity, depravity, or treason, and shall be punished by the sentence handed down by authorities in the Represidential Capital and contained in those paragraphs of the penal code concerning Treason Against the State or Treason Against the Represident, or Whispering, whichever shall be most severe.

52

THE ASSAULT

At the first deafening *Clang!* the Army of National Euphoria falls in. In precise, preplanned formation its soldiers
march toward the National Patriotic Square. Each soldier,
in his or her quadrangular battalion, stares fixedly at the
neck ahead. And so on, to the back of the formation, so
that the soldier responsible for internal intelligence sees but
one neck in each file. Now they are marching past me, with
their eyes fixed on the neck before them, softly murmuring
what they have received orders to repeat aloud whenever
the captain of each formation, in turn ordered by the colo-
nel of the great human blackboard, gives the signal. A
breath of excrement, of piss and sweat rises to my nose as
the vermin, in their uniform uniforms, approach, rhythmically, in their march to the Square. I look at them. They
come to the Square, formation by formation, and they take
their assigned places. From all the rooftops, parapets, and
watchtowers of the city the glorious anthems ring out in
homage to the Represident, who has not yet made his ap-
pearance. The first beasts of the first rank of each formation
raise a rag on which, in signs and figures, praise to the Represident is written. They keep marching in. Through the
smell of sweat and the *crack-crack* of bones crushed together in the mass of bodies I search for the miserable bitch.
Through all those claws and shaved heads I look for her
eyes filled with hate, so that I can liquidate her once and
for all. But she has still not come, so I go on scrutinizing
them, one by one—which is not difficult, since they are in
perfect order. It is exactly noon, and almost everyone is now

in place in his authorized area. The sound of the anthems rolls like thunder over the creaking and crackling of the crushed bones, the stench, the heat, and the dust. At a signal from the leader of the human blackboard, we National Heroes and other luminaries file in to take our places on the Secondary, Tertiary, Fourth- and subsequent-Degree Represidential Reviewing Stands. My grade of heroism puts me in the Fourth-Degree Stand. Beside me a Hero with the face of a rat is sitting, and when he looks at me he makes a sort of hoarse bleat. I ask him, very softly, what deeds he has done to merit this great honor. But the stinking pig keeps making that hoarse bleating sound. I realize that *that* was what qualified him: he has completely forgotten the language.

On the other side of me, I have a woman, or something that I think is supposed to be a woman. Its totally shaved head, its gray, wrinkled skin, its hands like dry wood, its dull, dead eyes without eyelashes, and its lips like two stark cracks in its face keep me from being certain what sex it belongs to. It is only the overalls without a fly that lead me to deduce that this is a woman. What magnificent deed, I wonder, must that petrified face have done, how many vermin must it have strangled, how many denounced? Or perhaps its heroism is even more edifying, perhaps this is one of the first to eat human flesh, or to donate its children to the Children's Cooperative, or come down with a fatal disease so as to infect some specific Enemy of the People. I discover that on this Fourth-Degree Reviewing Stand are the truly most heroic members of the Nation. The Second-Degree Reviewing Stand is occupied by old men and women and workers most of whom are deaf and blind from the constant, monotonous work they do. On the Third-Degree Stand are those that are not there to hear the Representident but rather to serve as a barrier between him and the rest of us. The degree of fanaticism of those particular swine is such that even agents of the Counterwhispering Corps fear them. And as for the First-Degree Reviewing

Stand, it is occupied entirely by ministers and vice-ministers, by ultra-ministers and post-ministers, and by vice-secretaries and pre-secretaries. And then, on a high platform, the High Secretary's box, and then at last, at the highest point of all, the Represident's Supreme Stage.

I observe those who are standing and sitting on the First-Degree Reviewing Stand, their enormous potbellies, their jowls, their awkward squirming, twisting, and turning in expectation of the grand arrival. On one side, the delegation of experts in state secrets; in another group, those who have distinguished themselves in the wielding of the billy club and in bestowing the three symbolic bashes. This platoon of whinnying little mules over here is the Children of the Nation—that is, those children whose denunciations brought their traitorous parents to justice, patriotic children who at some time or other heard a complaint or a whine or a murmur from their parents, or even a sigh of fatigue. The Represident likes to invite this kind of hero to the Grand Assemblies. And he almost always dedicates a round of congratulatory applause to them in his speeches. Now millions of claws are raised toward the Grand National Reviewing Stand. The High Secretary has made his entrance. His tall, lanky, wrinkled figure marches forward through the sea of shaved heads which are lowered as he passes. The terrified respect commanded by this figure is almost greater than that for the Represident himself. The High Secretary has never spoken publicly, but everyone knows his immense secret power, the endless cunning that has allowed him to survive in his position and not be annihilated by the Represident. And since the limits of his power are unknown, he is even more feared, and more fearsome. Now he comes at last to his place on the Grand National Reviewing Stand. When he bows in greeting (or perhaps in contemptuous condescension, though probably just because the height of the reviewing stand requires him to bend a bit if he is to look down upon the assembled masses), the silence that falls is absolute. The High Secretary contemplates that infinite sea of shaved heads for a few seconds, and then, at a signal from him, all the claws raised in his honor fall. I look at every one of those animals standing stiff and rigid—dazzled, or entranced, or secretly enraged—looking up toward the height at which we are stationed above them. On that human blackboard, the shaved heads form these words: GREATEST GLORY TO THE HEROES OF OUR GLORIOUS NATION. The High Secretary looks down at the message, which immediately dissolves to form another: WITH THE REPRESIDENT EVERYTHING, WITHOUT THE REPRESIDENT NOTHING. The High Secretary looks down again at the huge square, and his old cracked and dried lips almost seem to widen in a smile. EVERY WORD, EVERY GESTURE, EVERY MOVEMENT MADE SHOULD BE MADE TO THE GREATER GLORY OF OUR GLORIOUS NATION AND ITS METAGLORIOUS REPRESIDENT. And now that the last delegations have taken their places, the great human blackboard, with all its shaved heads, forms the gigantic words: LONG LIVE OUR GLORIOUS REPRESIDENT. The thunder of all the claws clacking at once is deafening. For more than an hour the entire Square applauds. I look, but none of these applauding vermin is my mother. I do not see her among the members of the human blackboard. I turn my long-range vision on the High Secretary. He is looking at me, too, through his binoculars. I seem to see his lips stretch a bit wider, and his eyes make a sort of sign to me. But it is all so fast that I cannot be sure. I look at him again, but he is just a lanky, dried-out old man standing in ecstasy before the immense sea of rodents.

At last the pre-anthems begin, and the figure of the Represident appears. Now the entire free universe is a snapping of flags and banners, a waving about of posters, placards, and signs, a flapping of rags, all wielded by the teeth of the multitude, and a storm of claws raised into the air, applauding deliriously. The languageless man beside me gives out a long howl of adoration. The apparent woman remains still and quiet, but from its eyes two great tears begin to roll down its cracked and furrowed face. And now the notes of the Represident's personal anthem begin to exert their calming effect on the immense crowd. At a gesture of his claws, the millions of shaved heads are bowed, and the tips of millions of noses touch the ground. Then the multitude stands at attention, observing the Minute of Silence. And now they bow down again and the only sound that is heard is the sound of their nervous breathing and the soft brushing of their dewlaps against the ground. Above the prostrate multitude the flags are still flying, the placards and posters waving like some strange animate beast. The Represident carries his great belly up to the highest point on the Grand National Reviewing Stand, and with his enormous binoculars he looks down on the subject hordes below him; his huge belly swells even larger in pride. As the anthem plays on, he continues to strut about on his monumental legs and buttocks, he turns his huge neck this way and that, he flaps his jowls (almost hidden within the thick wilderness of his beard), and he puffs and wheezes. . . .

At a gesture from the Represident the anthem ends. The loudspeakers announce that the Immortal Historic Moment has arrived, that the Represident will now bestow the Represidential Order of Highest Heroism, the medal bearing the Represident's own glorious likeness, upon the most outstanding heroes of our day. *The Sacrifice will follow this presentation*, the loudspeakers boom, *since if it were performed first, there is fear that the patriots sacrificed voluntarily by the masses and laid at the feet of the Represident might prevent the heroes from reaching the Reviewing Stand. . . .*

The first person to come to the Grand National Reviewing Stand is an ash-colored old man with a perfectly clean-shaven head. His heroism is truly magnificent; it consists of having memorized every word of every represidential speech, including the anthems, laws, slogans, and even the comic and ironic passages—in fact, every word ever publicly pronounced by Our Leader. The shaky, uncertain figure at last finishes his climb. The Represident raises one of his great claws and pins the medal to the old man's chest. The ash-colored old man's emotion is so great that the agents have to carry him off the stand on a stretcher. Now comes the furrow-faced apparent woman, and it turns out that she did in fact, just as I had supposed, contract every infectious disease known to man and spread them among our enemies. Leaving a trail of slimy suppuration, she climbs to the high tribunal, and the Represident, pulling on huge rubber gloves, pins the great medal on her chest, at arm's length. The woman collapses. The euphoria of the crowd is absolute. At a quick gesture from the Represident, several agents run to scoop up the newest hero, who has melted into pus-colored liquid and pestilential odor, and bear her away.

The loudspeakers continue with the presentations. Now, representing all those glorious children who placed Love of Country before Love of Family, the three Model Children are called to the platform. These are the children who will be decorated on behalf of all the rest. And the three little mules march up to the reviewing platform and come to attention before the immense hairy figure that is about to pin the medals on them. The faces of these three little pigs seem to be scanning all the faces on the platform, on all the other reviewing stands, and throughout the crowd below. They even examine the face of the Represident himself. There is nothing false or studied about these little animals; all their actions are solemnly conscious, monstrously genuine. They belong to this world, they are not of the past. The Represident himself is for them a product of another world, a world they would not hesitate one moment to annihilate, if necessary, in order to preserve this new world the Represident has made it possible to create. The insolence in their walk, as they now descend, seems to announce to all: *We three little pigs are above you all. Watch out, because we are the New Man. . . .*

The fanfares blare, announcing the next to be decorated, and at once all the flags, banners, pennants, placards, posters, etc. (how the hell should I know what all those things are called?) are raised in honor of *me*. I begin to ascend the steps to the high stage. Since it is a great distance from my Fourth-Degree Reviewing Stand to the pinnacle at which the Represident stands, I take advantage of the march to look closely at the faces of the packed crowd, searching for the face of my mother. The smell of shit and sweat is even greater now, since we are in the middle of the ceremony. As I breathe in that smell, I realize that I have been foiled again. And now, as I am coming closer and closer to the great central stage, the noise of the anthems sounds cruelly mocking to me, and my rage, my desire to kick out, can barely be controlled. But I continue on, until I bump into the tall, stooped figure of the High Secretary, who with a sinister gesture shows me the way to the represidential dais. I look with hatred at the worn figure of the High Secretary, like some featherless, battered bird, and I try to tell him that he has deceived me. But the anthems grow louder and louder, and the High Secretary, impassive, shows me the grand stairway that leads up to the topmost point on the reviewing stand.

As I climb, I give a last scrutinizing look at the crowd. My last look of disgust and revulsion at those millions of insects roasting in the sun, bowing, clacking their claws, and bowing again, without relief or consolation. Now the anthems fade away, signaling that the ceremony is to continue. Enraged, in the midst of the glare, while the slogans written across the human blackboard dizzyingly change (GLORY TO OUR GLORIOUS REPRESIDENT becomes LONG LIVE THE REPRESIDENT), I come to the topmost level of the Grand National Reviewing Stand, so high and so immense that it is like some great plateau from which one looks down upon the swaying, writhing sea of vermin below.

And there, on the precipice of that high plateau, he stands—that big-bellied, hairy, gigantic figure—with his back to me, like some turtle in its shell standing erect and in ecstasy before a sea of slaves. The jingling roll of a cymbal, or tiny gong, or cracker tin, or how the hell should I know what it is, announces the arrival of the new honoree. And then, a wave of his claw cutting off that hateful jangle, the huge backside turns, the protruding belly swings around toward me, and I am facing that enormous doughlike mound of flesh that holds in its claws the sparkling medal which is to be bestowed upon me. I know that the terrible solemnity of the moment demands that I lower my eyes and kiss his claw-feet. But still standing, rigid and furious, I raise my eyes to his face. And I see it, see that snout, see her snout—I see *her.* That face before me is the hated and horrible face of my mother. And it is also the face of the Represident. They are the same person. *That* is why it has been so hard to find her, I think, in fury. My surprise, my enraged joy, is so great that it takes me a second or two to recover.

The immense figure remains stiff, rigid, at the center of that great stage. The two of us stand there a moment, looking at each other, surprised and furious.

"So *that's* why I couldn't find you," I whisper, and I begin to walk toward her. She, attired in full regalia, steps back. Down below one can hear the waves of applause. The human blackboard traces out the words THE REPRESI-DENT IS INFINITE. The loudspeakers announce: *Now the Represident is about to present to the Hero of the Anti-Depravation and National Purification Legion his medal of honor . . .* I step closer and closer, while her steps take her backwards, clumsily, toward the rear of the high platform. She seems to be making surreptitious signals to the High Secretary and to the people standing on the Second-Degree Reviewing Stand. But I am getting closer. And as I walk toward her, my member, for the first time, begins to rise and stiffen. It grows so hard that it scrapes the fabric of my official multi-overalls, and vibrating tensely, breaks free. Swollen with fury, it takes aim at my mother. She staggers backward in terror, as the drums and cymbals and anthems echo like terrible thunder. Then recovering her composure, she picks up in her monumental claws one of her maces, or swords, or scepters, or canes, or whatever the fuck those things are called, and she hurls it at me furiously. I catch the iron whatever-it-is in the air, and I throw it into the wild crowd below, who no doubt think this is some entertaining new part of the ceremony. With my member ever harder and more erect, I continue to stalk her. She then grabs up a huge gear wheel of some kind, whirls it around dizzyingly, and launches it at my head. I dodge, and the wheel falls massively into the fearless (or petrified) crowd below, decapitating more than a hundred rats, which fall in formation. I am getting closer and closer, but she now grabs a huge, heavy sphere, which she hurls it at me like a discus. The gigantic ball falls, with a noise like the end of the earth, on the ministers' and vice-ministers' reviewing stand, killing them every one. While all the onlookers watch the struggle in paralyzed silence, my phallus throbs and rises, in greater and greater fury. And now it is touching the great she-mule, and as it strikes her chestful of medals, it knocks off her protective shell. A hail of medals, ribbons, tinkling pieces of tin, sashes and pins, badges and other decorations falls off her. Now utterly beside herself with rage, she somehow lays her hands on an immense whip plaited out of something that looks like sharp, lead-colored snakes, and she whirls it about and snaps it in the air, and then she lashes it at me, felling the Heroic Children and all the rest of the mob of heroes that preceded them.

I have never been so aroused. I stand with my legs apart, my face as flushed in fury as my phallus, and I take aim at her and charge. Her second layer of armor falls in a tinkling rain over the transfixed crowd. She fires a hail of gigantic spikes at me, but they strike the heroes on the Third-Degree Reviewing Stand. I am so enraged (one of the spikes grazed me) that I charge her again, this time with my phallus even more inflamed. And her third skin of armor falls off her. Cornered, but still trying to finish me off, she opens a valve inside her uniform, and a jet of boiling-hot steam shoots out, but with a terrible noise like grinding gears it sprays all the heroes of the Fourth-Degree and Fifth-Degree Reviewing Stands. I scramble behind her, and under the cover afforded me by the mounds of her enormous buttocks I leap over her, land before her, and continue my attack. With one blow, my member knocks off her fourth coat of armor. And at last I can see her head without its protective helmet—that hated head of a cunning old hag, her ash-colored mat of hair like some stinking nanny goat's emitting a stench of sweat and fury. I also see her mouth, her horrible mouth, which once even pronounced my name. And looking at that smirk, that horrible hypocritical smirk, those eyes that are still looking at me in that superior way of hers, my fury and my erection grow even more terribly uncontrollable, and aiming my phallus directly at her heart, I attack. Her fifth and sixth layers of armor fall, but she turns and runs, hurling claws and metal objects and pieces of wood behind her, and snarling and snapping her teeth. I charge her again, and her last coat of armor falls off and rolls down the steps into the crowd. And now I see her— she is there before me, covered with blotches and wrinkles. She is naked. Her huge buttocks and breasts, her body like some monstrous toad's, her ash-gray hair and her stinking hole are exposed for all to see. With my member throbbingly erect, and my hands on my hips, I stand before her, looking at her. My hatred and my revulsion and my arousal are now beyond words to describe.

And then the great cow, naked and horrible, white and stinking, plays her last card; the sly bitch, crossing her ragged claws over her monstrous breasts, looks at me with tears in her eyes and she says *Son*. That is all I can bear to hear. All the derision, all the harassment, all the fear and frustration and blackmail and mockery and contempt that that word contains—it slaps me in the face, and I am stung. My erection swells to enormous proportions, and I begin to step toward her, my phallus aimed dead for its mark, that fetid, stinking hole. And I thrust. As she is penetrated, she gives a long, horrible shriek, and then she collapses. I sense my triumph—I come, and I feel the furious pleasure of discharging myself inside her. Howling, she explodes in a blast of bolts, washers, screws, pieces of shrapnellike tin, gasoline, smoke, semen, shit, and streams of motor oil. Then, at the very instant of my climax, and of her final howl, a sound never heard before washes across the immense square below us. A deafening whisper, uttered by every member of the crowd, begins to move across the Square, destroying everything in its path, killing every agent whose ears it reaches. And then, suddenly, that mass of vermin that a moment before stood transfixed begins to claw, and it claws down the reviewing stands, the watchtowers, and the parapets. Seizing the poles on which the flags of the Nation had flown, the crowd begins to march, razing all that stands before it, pulling down the Multi-Families, the not-parks, the loudspeakers, and the Cells on Wheels. The destruction is so terrible that even the whispering itself, which grows louder and louder, is muted by the noise of objects falling and crashing, bones cracking, rooftop emplacements and placards, Heroic Countenances and iron bars creaking and popping and smashing to bits.

While the crowd goes on moving through the city, hunting down and destroying to the accompaniment of the music of its own enraged whispering, I tuck the limp mass of my phallus (now at last spent and flaccid) into my overalls. Weary, I make my way unnoticed through the noise and the riot (the crowd in a frenzy of destruction, like children, crying *The Represent is dead, the beast at last is dead!*), and I come to the wall of the city. I walk down to the shore. And I lie down in the sand.

The various original Spanish-language versions of El asalto *may be found among Reinaldo Arenas' manuscripts in the Firestone Library, Princeton University, Princeton, New Jersey.*